Festivals and Customs

Patricia Morrell

Festivals and Customs

illustrated by Peter Clark

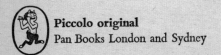
Piccolo original
Pan Books London and Sydney

First published 1977 by Pan Books Ltd,
Cavaye Place, London SW10 9PG
© Patricia Morrell 1977
ISBN 0 330 25215 1
Printed and bound in Great Britain by
Richard Clay (The Chaucer Press) Ltd, Bungay, Suffolk

Contents

January

January is the first month of the year, and it takes its name from the old Roman god called Janus. Janus took care of all the beginnings, and doors and gates were given into his special care. In very old sculptures and carvings he was often to be found with two faces, one at the front of his head and another at the back, so that he was able to look both ways at once.

The old Romans called him the keeper of the door, and thought of him as a kindly god who would open the door to let the old year out and the new year in. (The word

janitor, meaning door-keeper, also comes from the name of this ancient god.)

Here is an old rhyme which helps us to remember how many days there are in each month:

Thirty days hath September,
April, June and November.
All the rest have thirty-one,
Excepting February alone,
Which has but twenty-eight days clear,
And twenty-nine in each leap year.

New Year's Eve

Beginning the year with New Year's Eve, which is 31 December, may seem rather strange, but in the past people believed that the last hours of the old year were very important. It was a time to make good resolutions for the year to come, and to put away all bad habits and begin afresh.

Certain customs and celebrations are observed on this night, and in many towns and villages church bells ring out at midnight to welcome the new year. Some churches have a special service at midnight, called a 'Watch Night Service', and people sing carols and hymns together. In some country districts there may be a supper afterwards, held at the church hall or in an inn close by.

In Ireland candles are lit and placed in the windows of the churches and houses, as a sign of welcome to the new year. In certain parts of Ireland they will even light twelve candles, one for each of the twelve apostles, and these will burn until the eve of Twelfth Night.

New Year's Eve in Scotland is called Hogmanay, and the Scottish people celebrate this event even more than they do Christmas. 'Hogmanay' is a very old Scottish word that is thought to come from the old custom of housewives leaving tiny helpings of bread or cake on their doorsteps for the fairy folk. By taking care not to offend the little people, it was hoped that they would watch over the house in the year to come, and ensure that there would be peace and prosperity for everyone.

'First footing' is another old Scottish custom that is kept up in many parts of the world. The first foot over the threshold is said to determine the luck of the year, and traditionally it must be a dark-haired man who comes first footing. He must carry with him some sort of gift for the household, often a piece of coal, or a small loaf of bread, or maybe some salt, indicating that there will be food and warmth in plenty in the house all through the year.

In New Zealand they keep up the old custom of first footers, particularly where Scottish people have settled, and after the ceremony there is usually a big family party with friends and neighbours, and dancing and games for everyone.

In Australia they too have big New Year parties and family reunions, but unlike us with our damp cold climate, they are able to set up party tables in the garden and have barbecues. Their weather is very warm at this time of year, and it is not uncommon to find that the gardens are full of twinkling fairy lights, and that the smaller shrubs and trees have been hung with gaily coloured baubles and tinsel.

New Year's Day
There are not so many celebrations for New Year's Day
as there used to be, even though the day is now a public
holiday.

There used to be an old custom of bringing something
into the house on New Year's Day before anything was
allowed to be taken out, even if it was only a dustpan of
ashes that needed to be taken out. The mistress of the
house would caution her servants that if any household
rubbish or ashes were removed from the house before the
second day of January, it would mean instant dismissal for
them. Neighbours would bring small gifts to each other
on New Year's Day. Amongst poorer families the gift
would probably be just a small jug of milk, or maybe a
log of wood, but wealthier people would bring more
lavish gifts, and all the gifts would serve to set the luck for
the year. This tradition is now almost forgotten.

Handsel Monday
Handsel Monday is the first Monday in January, and it
follows an ancient Scottish custom. This was the day
when tradesmen who delivered to the house could expect
to receive small gifts of money as a token of thanks.

Handsel Monday was once a holiday, and farming
people gave their workers a feast. This old tradition died
out around the beginning of the eighteenth century, but
in some country districts small gifts are still given. The
name of Handsel gifts comes from an old Scandinavian
word that means 'to give into the hand'.

Twelfth Night

The sixth day of January is the last day of Christmas, and usually on this day we take down all the Christmas decorations and carry out the evergreens. Our ancestors were very superstitious and used to burn all their decorations, for they believed that evil spirits and witches might have hidden away in them with the intention of haunting the house and bringing bad luck in the year ahead.

This day is also the feast of the Epiphany, which is remembered as the day when the Three Wise Men first saw the bright star in the east, and were guided by its light to the stable in Bethlehem. In some parts of northern France, children still celebrate the ancient custom of going out on Epiphany Eve to meet the kings on their travels, and to look for the bright star of old.

There used to be a Twelfth Night or Epiphany cake and it was the custom for the maker to put into the cake a wedding ring and a button. When the cake was cut the person who received the wedding ring knew that he or she would marry soon, but whoever received the button could count on remaining single. This old tradition has now completely gone in this country, although it is still known in France, and the only traditional cake we have is the Christmas cake. The French Epiphany cake (or Bean cake) is a very rich cake often decorated with gold and silver ornaments depicting the Three Wise Men.

Festivities in the past for Twelfth Day used to begin on the eve of Twelfth Night. In country areas these festivities were of great importance because the success or failure of the new crops was thought to be dependent upon the way they were carried out. At dusk large bonfires were lit in the fields, and it was customary for the farmer and his men to encircle the bonfires and drink to the health of the farm in cider or ale. There would be much shouting and singing for they believed that the more noise they made the more chance there would be of the evil spirits being scared off.

After the bonfire there would be a huge supper in the farmhouse kitchen, and when the feasting was over everyone went out into the darkness again to visit the stables and the cattle pens. Here they would all drink to the health of the cattle, and of every living beast that the farm possessed, with the same purpose in mind – to keep the farm free from all forms of evil and to ensure prosperity.

Plough Monday

The first Monday after Twelfth Day is Plough Monday, and years ago in country districts there were important ceremonies and rites connected with it.

Plough Monday was the day when the church was asked to bless all the agricultural workers and their land. The plough would be decorated with greenery and dragged by farm workers through the streets to the church to receive the priest's blessing. In some villages the farm workers made the day a holiday and would dress up in gay clothes, hang the plough with ribbons and flowers, and after the plough had been blessed by the church they would drag it around the streets visiting each inn to beg for ale or cider to complete their merrymaking.

Candles would burn in the churches in honour of the saints, prayers would be offered asking for good crops during the coming year, and those poor people who could not afford to buy candles for the church would beg money from the richer members of the congregation. This custom died a natural death, however, because the temptation to spend the candle money on ale and cider became almost universal, and Plough Monday became just another riotous occasion.

It was during the middle of the last century that this rustic festival died out, but in recent years attempts have been made to bring it back. In some churches now a special service is held on the first Monday after the Epiphany, and the plough will be brought into the church and blessed – just as it was all those years ago.

Old Twelfth Night

January 17 is Old Twelfth Night, and is still celebrated in many parts of Somerset. It is a ceremony with a pagan origin, the object being to drive away all evil spirits from the cider apple orchards.

The villagers gather together early in the evening and form a circle around the largest apple tree. Then the men fire guns through the branches, and cider is thrown over the trunk of the tree, and sometimes pieces of toast or cake soaked in cider are placed in the forks of the tree. This is done each year to thank the gods of the trees for their protection during the last year, and further to ensure that their year's apple harvest will be a good one.

It is all part of the ceremony for the children to rattle and bang saucepan lids together and make a fearful din. Again it is intended to frighten off any evil-doers who might be lurking around the trees. To finish off this old rite, everyone taking part will sing the old wassail song and drink cider in a toast to the trees.

Here's to thee, old apple tree,
Whence thou mayst bud,
Whence thou may blow,
And whence thou mayst bear apples enow,
Hats full!
Caps full!
And our pockets full too!
Hurrah! Hurrah!

Burns' Night

This Scottish festival will usually take place on 25 January, or on the nearest possible date convenient. It is held in honour of the famous Scottish poet Robert Burns, whose birthday was on 25 January. He died in 1796 from rheumatic fever, at the young age of thirty-seven.

Robert Burns was often called the Ploughman Poet, because at one time he was a farm labourer. His small cottage in Alloway, Ayr, is now preserved as a museum, and was said to have been built by the poet's father. Burns became famous for his poems and ballads at the age of twenty-seven, and he wrote the words to that immortal Scottish air, 'Auld Lang Syne', the tune of which dates back a few more centuries. Burns earned a reputation as a rather dashing young man with a passion for living life to the full.

The Burns' Night dinner is a grand occasion. Many of the gentlemen wear kilts, and a haggis is piped in and is ceremonially cut with a dirk (a Scottish dagger). Many Scottish reels, country dances and jigs are performed, and it is a very festive occasion that has now become worldwide wherever Scottish people have settled.

St Paul's Day

St Paul's Day falls on 25 January, and this was once another important day in the old countryman's year. It was on this day that farmers and country people took stock of the weather. A long-range weather forecast was devised for the year to come, and everyone took this very seriously and planned their farming year accordingly.

This is an old rhyme concerning St Paul's Day:

If the day of St Paul be cleare,
There shall betide a happie year,
If it do chance to snow or rain,
Then shall be deare all kinde of graine,
But if the winde then bee alofte,
Warres shall vex this realm full oft,
And if the clouds make dark the skie,
Both neate and fowle this yeare shall die.

Why St Paul was singled out for these honours is not clearly known, although it may be connected with St Paul's foretelling of stormy weather and a rough passage during a voyage to Rome that ended in a shipwreck.

Australia Day

Although 26 January is Australia Day, it is usually celebrated on the Monday closest to that date. On this day Australians commemorate the beginning of their country, for on 26 January 1788 the first eleven ships arrived at Botany Bay from England. The voyage had been long and hazardous, taking eight months, with some of the ships holding deported convicts and some carrying ordinary people wanting to make a new life for themselves. At first the settlers found many setbacks with soil that was poor and with crops often failing, but after the early days of hardship new farms and towns gradually began to flourish. Today Australia is the world's biggest producer and exporter of wool, and is also rich in gold and famous for its cattle and wheat.

Australia Day is a festive day all over Australia, with everyone having a holiday. The streets in most states are gaily decorated with flags and banners, and there are carnivals and sometimes air displays, and children act in short plays at their schools.

February

February is the shortest month of the year with only twenty-eight days, but with twenty-nine days when leap year falls. (The earth circles round the sun once in every year, taking $365\frac{1}{4}$ days to do so. The extra quarter days are added together every fourth year, thus making one extra day which is inserted into the calendar as 29 February. And so every fourth year will be a leap year, and will have 366 days.)

An old superstition tells us that when 29 February comes round in the leap years, ladies may propose marriage to men. It is also said that if the gentleman is

unwilling and refuses the offer, he is expected to buy the lady a new dress.

Candlemas Day

The second day of February is Candlemas Day, sometimes known as the Feast of Candles. In Roman Catholic countries this is a festival to commemorate the purification of the Virgin Mary, whilst other churches commemorate the day when Jesus was taken to the temple in Jerusalem to be presented to the priests.

Another explanation for this festival is that it celebrates the return of light after the dark winter months, being halfway between the longest night and the spring equinox.

For the Feast of Candles, candles are brought to the church and lighted during the Church service, and blessed by the priests. This is done in accordance with the belief that a 'hallowed' candle (a candle that has been blessed) kept in the home will act as a deterrent against all forms of evil and witchcraft.

This day also used to be the absolutely final day for removing Christmas decorations, if this had not been done on Twelfth Night. Otherwise goblins or witches would have the power to enter the household and take up residence, perhaps remaining there undetected for the rest of the year, working evil and mischief on the unfortunate inhabitants.

Farmers were very superstitious too, and were well pleased if Candlemas Day dawned fine and clear so that they could take heart from this rhyme:

If Candlemas Day be fine and cleare,
Corn and fruit will then be deare.

Waitangi Day

Waitangi Day is 6 February and is New Zealand's national day of commemoration and thanksgiving for the signing of the Treaty of Waitangi in 1840. This treaty established peace between the Maori natives and the new settlers, settled disputes about the division of land, and all the residents of the New Zealand Islands became British subjects, including 395 Maori chiefs.

Waitangi Day was made a public holiday in 1973, so New Zealanders are now able to celebrate the day in style.

St Valentine's Day

On 14 February we celebrate St Valentine's Day by sending Valentine cards to our sweethearts. This custom is popular in many countries, with special cards available from shops. In Canada many schoolchildren make their own cards, and have special parties and dances to celebrate the day.

Valentine himself was a priest who lived in Rome around the third century AD. He was beheaded for giving shelter to some Christians who were in danger of being persecuted. His death came at the same time of year as the Romans celebrated an old pagan festival of 'love feasts and lotteries'. At this festival it was the custom for all the unmarried women and men to draw lots from an urn, and the name that they drew out would be the name of the person they would keep company with for the year ahead.

This lottery was very popular, and in later years the Christian church tried hard to do away with the custom. But this proved to be impossible, so they compromised and instead dedicated the feasts and lotteries to a

Christian saint. St Valentine was chosen simply because the time of his martyrdom coincided most conveniently with the love feasts. He really had no connection with lovers or feasts.

Birds are supposed to pair off for mating on St Valentine's Day, so this might be the reason why so many of the old Valentine cards were elaborately decorated with turtle doves and love birds. Gentlemen would often give their Valentines expensive gifts, such as extravagant pieces of jewellery or costly gowns. Gradually, however, the value of Valentine gifts diminished, until by the mid nineteenth century only elaborate cards with sentimental verse were being sent.

A little later Valentine cards were sent anonymously, so that sometimes the real sender was never discovered. Today we still keep up the custom of sending cards, but today's cards are often more light-hearted than the cards with sentimental verse so beloved of our Victorian ancestors.

One old superstition once connected with this day, but seldom heard these days, is that the first unmarried man to be seen by a single girl on St Valentine's Day is destined to be her future husband.

Shrove Tuesday

Shrove Tuesday is better known to most of us as Pancake Day. It is nearly always in February, although its actual date is determined by the date of Easter. Easter is a movable feast (as explained in the chapter on 'April') so the date will vary each year. Shrove Tuesday is the day before Ash Wednesday, the day on which Lent begins.

In the past people had a holiday on Shrove Tuesday, with children allowed a day off school. Merrymaking went on in the streets as people took advantage of the fact that it was the last day before the beginning of Lent, during which all feasting and fun would cease. Children would go from door to door begging for sweets and other delicacies, and there might be such sports as bear-baiting and cock-fighting going on. It was generally a riotous time, so that quieter people were glad when Lent did actually start.

During Lent most Christians kept very strictly to a simple diet, often just of bread and water. So on Shrove Tuesday housewives used up all the food that would be forbidden before Lent began. Not wishing to waste precious eggs, fats, flour and milk, thrifty housewives evolved the idea of mixing all these ingredients together, pouring the mixture into a pan, and cooking it slowly

over a fire. It was difficult to turn this large 'cake' in the pan, so the art of tossing pancakes had to be developed.

Nowadays one of the most famous Shrovetide customs is the pancake tossing at Westminster School. Here, a large pancake is carried into the great hall in a frying pan and is tossed by the cook very high in the air. As it falls the boys scramble for it, and the boy who manages to get the biggest piece is rewarded with a prize.

Then there are the pancake races at Olney, a custom said to be more than five hundred years old. Only women may take part in this race, and they must wear a hat or scarf and an apron – it is forbidden to wear slacks. Each lady has a frying pan containing a pancake which should still be cooking, according to the rules. She has to toss the pancake three times during the actual race, which starts at the market square and ends at the church door. The first lady to reach the door where the vicar and bellringer are waiting is the winner. She receives the prize of a prayer-book from the vicar, and usually gets a kiss from the bellringer.

This race apparently originated from the year 1445, in the days when a 'shriving bell' was rung to summon the people to church on Shrove Tuesday. One woman of Olney was still busy using up her eggs and milk by making them into a pancake when she heard the bell ring. She ran to church still in her apron, and still clutching the frying pan.

A similar race takes place on the same day in Liberal, Kansas, USA. It seems that a friendly rivalry has sprung up between the two towns as to which can boast the fastest time. Liberal will ring up Olney immediately after the race to know of Olney's result, and to record their own. And – like the winner in Olney – the Liberal housewife will receive a prayer-book, and she gets a kiss from the member of the British Council for the area. There is also a travelling trophy between the two towns – it is an engraved pancake griddle that is held by the winning town each year.

Most Christian people went to church on Shrove Tuesday, to confess their sins before Lent began. Having confessed, the priest would pronounce them absolved or shriven and they felt they had prepared themselves for the solemn weeks ahead. This also gave them a sense of freedom, so that they could take part in the celebrations with a clear conscience.

Pancake Day is not so widely celebrated in Canada, where they specialize in two different kinds of pancakes – flapjacks and crêpes. Flapjacks are quite thick and are eaten with generous helpings of maple syrup or jam, whilst the crêpes are very thin and lacy. In the more isolated parts, such as on the prairie, boy scouts often take over the day's celebrations and sponsor a pancake supper. This is a good time for a neighbourly get-together, as are the pancake races in some of the towns, where one street races against the other.

Ash Wednesday

This is the Wednesday after Shrove Tuesday, and is the first day of Lent. After all the feasting and merrymaking on Shrove Tuesday, Ash Wednesday must have seemed a very solemn quiet day for our ancestors. The long fast began in memory of the forty days that Christ spent in the wilderness. Many people wore black clothes on Ash Wednesday, and it was observed as a day of mourning. Everyone went to church, and during the service the priests would sprinkle ashes on the heads of the congregation as a reminder of the fact that they were all sinners, and must do penance for their sins.

Throughout Lent the Church tried to influence their followers, insisting that meat must only be eaten on Sundays with only plain food allowed during the rest of the week, such as a little fish or maybe some eggs. Even today we still hear of Christians 'giving up' something for Lent, such as sweets or some other luxury enjoyed at normal times.

Jack o' Lent

This old custom is scarcely heard of today, but in medieval times it was very popular.

A straw figure was made and dressed in rags, and was

intended to represent Judas Iscariot, the disciple who betrayed Christ. This ragged figure was paraded through the streets on Ash Wednesday through crowds of booing and jeering people. It was then placed in a prominent position where everyone could see it, and those who wished to, threw sticks and stones at it all through the period of Lent. If anything at all remained of this quaint figure when Lent was finished, it would be burnt publicly. Most often there was very little left to burn.

March

March is usually a bustling month with very cold winds and some strong gales. There is an old saying about this month which seems most appropriate:

March comes in like a lion,
But goes out like a lamb.

March is named after Mars, the Roman god of war. The Romans gave the month its name, intending it to be a compliment to themselves as they were great warriors and liked to be known as 'the sons of war'.

St David's Day

St David is the patron saint of Wales, and St David's Day is celebrated on 1 March. St David lived in the sixth century, and he was a great preacher who constantly encouraged his people in times of hardship. There are many old legends told about him and the wonderful things that he did.

St David was said to have lived to a great age, and was thought to be 140 years old when he died. People apparently grieved so much for him at his death that where their tears fell, leeks sprung up! There are several old legends about the Welsh leek and how it became the Welsh emblem, and many of them are concerned with the saint himself.

One old story tells us that St David was once fighting with his people in a battle against an intruding army, and

the two armies became so intermingled that it was extremely difficult to tell friend from foe. As they were fighting in a field of leeks at the time, St David cried out to his people, 'Pick the leeks, and wear them in your helmets, so that you may know one another.' Welsh regiments are still to this day presented with leeks on St David's Day.

Another tale concerning the saint and leeks tells how St David lived a very simple life, existing mainly on the frugal diet of bread and leeks. Because of his wonderful understanding and compassion for his people, everyone thought that the leeks he ate must surely possess magical properties to give him these qualities that they themselves lacked.

The daffodil vies with the leek as a national emblem of Wales, and is often worn in buttonholes on St David's Day as well as appearing on coins and stamps. The daffodil was first brought to Wales by the Spaniards, who exchanged it with the old Druids for anthracite. Because of its brilliant yellow colouring the Druids looked upon it as a sacred flower and called it 'The Flower of the Sun'.

Moomba Festival

In Melbourne, Australia, 10 March brings a big festival known as Moomba Festival. Moomba is an old Aborigine word meaning 'let's get together and have a good time'.

For one week Melbourne becomes 'Moomba City', and everyone celebrates and enjoys all the different entertainments. There are carnivals, marching bands, jazz concerts, folk music, and many kinds of large-scale exhibitions.

Everywhere there are gay thronging people who have

come into Melbourne for the festival. There are lots of exciting things for the children to do, but in particular they can have rides in the glittering Moomba Show Boat called *Queen of the Pacific* which is on the Yarra river. There are water-ski championships, a water carnival, and many swimming contests, Australian children being very keen swimmers.

Melbourne is a very beautiful city of which the Australians are justly proud, and at this time of year it will be filled with visitors all bent on enjoying this great festival. Moomba closes with a last colourful parade of floats and a dazzling evening display of fireworks which illuminates the whole city.

St Patrick's Day

St Patrick's Day is 17 March, and Irish people everywhere like to wear a sprig of shamrock in their buttonholes for this is a very special day for Ireland. St Patrick (who lived in the fifth century) is the patron saint of Ireland, and the shamrock is supposed to be his emblem.

There is a legend which tells how the shamrock first became the emblem of Ireland and it concerns the saint's difficulty, while preaching to his people on a hillside, of making them understand the meaning of the Holy Trinity, the Three in One. They just could not understand how three persons could be one God, so he looked about him for an example with which to show them. Growing at his feet he saw a small three-leaved plant which he picked and held up for all to see. He pointed out that the three separate little leaves of the tiny plant were still only one leaf, because they all grew from the same central point. In just the same way, he said, the three Holy Persons of the Trinity – Father, Son, and Holy Ghost – were all distinctive personalities, and yet were but one God. Ever since this day, the shamrock has been St Patrick's own special emblem.

Like all the saints, St Patrick has many old stories told about him, the most famous of which relates to how he rid Ireland of poisonous snakes and reptiles. It seems that Ireland was once a land thickly populated with reptiles, and there were so many that people went in fear of their lives. St Patrick was weary of seeing his people so frightened and distressed, and one day he decided to do something about it. He climbed to the top of a high mountain, and when he had reached the top he used all his saintly powers to draw the deadly snakes and reptiles up the mountain after him. He then drove them down the other side of the mountain, and kept on driving them until they had reached the sea, where they all perished. And to this very day, there are no snakes in Ireland.

It is customary for Irish people living abroad to wear a sprig of shamrock, or wear something green, on St Patrick's Day. During the St Patrick's Day dances and parties in Canada it has even been known for the beer to be coloured green in honour of the day.

St Patrick, who was reputed to have been well over a hundred years old when he died, was buried at Downpatrick, County Down, and many Irish people make a pilgrimage to his grave each year on 17 March. St Patrick's cross is a red diagonal on a white background, and it has been part of the British national flag since the early nineteenth century.

As well as being Ireland's own patronal festival, 17 March can claim another distinction. In medieval days it was

celebrated as the anniversary of the day when Noah and his family, complete with animals, entered the ark. In many parts of England plays and tableaux were presented, all concerned with Noah and his family and the building of the ark. But this old custom has long since gone, and it is doubtful whether anyone ever celebrates it nowadays.

Mothering Sunday

Mothering Sunday falls on the fourth Sunday in Lent, and it is usually around 28 March. In the past this was always a holiday for servant girls and apprentices learning their trades, when they were allowed the day off to visit their mothers. It was the custom for them to take a small present for their mothers, the girls perhaps gathering a posy of flowers from the hedgerows on the way, or baking a special cake, and the boys buying a small trinket.

The cakes they baked in the Middle Ages are now known as simnel cakes although their cakes were more like oversized mince pies than cakes. They were very different from today's simnel cakes, and were really pastry cases filled with fruits, candied peel and spices – they were very rich and filling.

There is an amusing little legend telling how the first simnel cake was made by an old couple known as Simon and Nell. They quarrelled violently as to whether this special cake should be boiled or baked, until eventually they compromised and decided to boil the cake for a little while first, and then to bake it in the oven for the remaining time it took to cook. And since they had both shared in the making of it, they decided to call it the Sim-Nell cake, which of course has long since been shortened to simnel.

Today we celebrate a Mothering Sunday service in our churches, and the children are often given small posies of flowers during the service to take home to their mothers.

On Mothering Sunday above all other,
Every child should dine with its mother.

April

In April everything begins to grow again: the buds open out on the trees, birds begin to sing once more, and all forms of life make a new start after the long dormant winter. The name April is taken from the Latin word *aperire*, which means 'to open out', and the Romans decided to dedicate this month to Venus, the goddess of beauty.

April Fool's Day

The first day of April is sometimes called April (or All) Fool's Day, and it is a day for playing tricks on everybody. Children especially enjoy this day because everyone can try to make other people look ridiculous; but no time must be wasted for at midday all things return to normal and all jokes and pranks must stop.

In the past, particularly in Victorian times, much more was made of April Fool's Day, and children would get up especially early to play tricks on everyone. A favourite trick was to cry out to someone that their shoelace was undone, and when they looked down to shout out loudly, 'April Fool!' Another old trick often played upon the youngest apprentice was to send him or her upon a false errand, to fetch something quite silly such as two penn'orth of common sense, and when of course they returned without it, to greet them with cries of, 'April Fool!'

In France, April Fool's Day is known as 'Poisson

d'Avril' – April Fish Day. Children will sometimes make a paper fish and try to attach it to the back of the coat or dress of a grown-up, and then dance along behind calling out, 'See the April Fish!'

There is no really satisfactory reason for celebrating 1 April like this, as the following rhyme says:

The first of April some folks say,
Is set apart for All Fool's Day,
But why the people call it so,
Nor I nor they themselves do know.

One explanation for these curious acts and silly pranks goes back to the time when kings and other important noblemen kept their own jesters or fools at court or in their castles. Fools were in those days a very necessary part of the household, because they kept the master of the house in a good humour by telling him jokes to make him laugh when he was sad, by soothing him with an air on the lute if he was tired, or simply by singing him a merry song. If all this failed to please, they would juggle or caper about performing all kinds of antics until the master began to smile again.

Jesters wore garments of many colours, and wore caps with long peaks from which usually hung small tinkling bells. They carried a stick with either a cockerel's head or a doll's head moulded to the end of it, and they would often pretend to carry on mock conversations with this head. Perhaps this is where the art of ventriloquism began.

It was said that once a year on 1 April the jesters were given a holiday until twelve o'clock midday, and other people in the court of household had to take over the exacting duties of the jester.

Another explanation of All Fool's Day is the story of Persephone, the goddess of spring, who was stolen away by the wicked king of the underworld. When her mother, Demeter, heard her daughter's screams she set off at once to find her. But her daughter did not answer her calls, and only the lonely echo of her own voice could be heard, and she was heard to say sadly that she had been 'on a fool's errand'.

Whatever the real reason behind this old custom it is still a merry day for children because it is the one day when they can enjoy catching adults out and making them look foolish.

The First Cuckoo
Besides bringing primroses and other lovely spring flowers, April brings the cuckoo. Around the 14th or 15th day of this month we can expect to hear the first

calls of the cuckoo, although cuckoos have once or twice been heard in March during exceptionally mild weather.

To hear the first call of the cuckoo is said to be very lucky, and it is a time to make a wish. Old legends tell us that a child born on the day the first cuckoo is heard will always be lucky.

Another charming old legend about the cuckoo tells of an old lady who is in charge of the cuckoos and lets them out at the Heathfield Fair on the 14th day of April. If she is feeling good-tempered she will release many birds, but should she be cross, then only one or two will have their freedom. And this strange factor is thought to have some bearing upon the weather. Few cuckoos is said to mean a rainy summer, but persistent calls from the bird is a sign of a long dry summer to come.

There are many legends and superstitions about the cuckoo, and although he is really a lazy bird who would much rather make use of the skylark's nest or the meadow pipit's than build one of his own he is still the messenger of summer. When we first hear his call across the woods and fields we can be sure that summer is not too far away.

In April come he will
In May he sings all day,
In June he'll change his tune,
In July he'll fly,
In August go he must.

Easter
Before beginning the Eastertide customs it is necessary to explain that although Easter sometimes comes in March, it more often falls in April, and so all the customs connected with it are usually considered in this month. It

was decided in the fourth century that the date of Easter should be on the first Sunday following the first full moon after the Vernal (or Spring) Equinox. Equinox means the time of year when the sun crosses the equator and day and night become equal in length. This generally takes place around 20 March so that Easter must fall somewhere between 22 March and 25 April.

Palm Sunday

The Eastertide customs begin on Palm Sunday, the Sunday before Easter Sunday. Before the Reformation in the sixteenth century, this day was celebrated with great processions of priests and choristers, monks and nuns, all walking through the streets carrying branches of palm. There would often be an ass in the procession with a

statue of Christ sitting upon its back, and the people watching would throw small crosses or branches of palm or willow in front of the ass as it passed, in remembrance of the children of Jerusalem who did this all those years ago on the first Palm Sunday.

Today some of our Churches still have the old custom of handing out small palm crosses on this day. In some parishes there may be a special children's service when the children follow a procession headed by the choir to the altar, where they each receive their crosses. The old tradition of keeping the crosses until the next year in a Bible or prayer-book is still observed by some.

Maundy Thursday

This is the Thursday before Good Friday in Holy Week, the name Maundy coming from an old Latin word, *mandatum*, meaning 'a command'. Maundy Thursday commemorates the eve of the Last Supper, and also commemorates Jesus washing the feet of his disciples after the supper was over. He told the disciples that by thus doing he had cleansed them from sin.

So the custom of washing the feet was carried on through the ages, with monks performing the disciples' task of cleansing the feet of the poor. But as time passed the ritual was altered, and it became customary for the reigning monarch to perform this very humble duty. James II was the last King of England to carry out this ceremony, for by the reign of William and Mary the custom had been delegated to the King's Almoner.

By the reign of Queen Victoria money was being distributed instead, and this is still done on each Maundy Thursday to this day. Usually the Queen or a member of the Royal Family will be present on this occasion, and the money is contained in small leather purses, either white or red. There are specially minted coins for this ceremony – silver penny, twopenny, threepenny and fourpenny coins – and people chosen to receive this money will each be given coins to the value of a penny for each year of the reigning sovereign's life.

All those taking part in the ceremony will carry a tiny posy of sweet herbs and flowers, and the members of the clergy have linen towels on their shoulders. This is a reminder of the time when the actual foot-washing did take place. (The posy of herbs and flowers is in memory of the traditional protection against the plague, for it must be remembered that the streets of any big city until the eighteenth century would have been littered with much foul-smelling and decaying refuse.)

Good Friday
From very early days the Church has set aside Good Friday as a day for fasting and mourning, because this is the day when the Crucifixion is remembered. This day is still commemorated, and today we have a national holiday in Britain.

Many of us eat spicy hot cross buns for breakfast. Street criers used to walk through the streets very early on Good Friday morning, selling freshly baked buns in baskets covered with a clean white cloth. They knocked on the doors or rang handbells to rouse the people to buy, and would cry out loudly:

One a penny buns,
Two a penny buns,
If you have no daughters,

Give them to your sons,
One a penny, two a penny,
Hot cross buns!

The old tradition of eating hot cross buns on Good
Friday is almost certainly linked with the consumption of
unleavened bread that was eaten by the Israelites on the
night when Moses led them out of their captivity in
Egypt. The early Christians continued to eat unleavened
bread (which is bread without yeast) at this time, but
gradually through the years the bread got smaller and
smaller until finally it resembled a bun rather than a loaf.
But they were always marked with a cross to serve as a
reminder of the Crucifixion, as indeed they still are to this
day.

Hot cross buns are eaten in other parts of the world, but
in far-flung parts of Australia such as Alice Springs the
buns would most probably be home-baked. Canadians
too have hot cross buns on Good Friday, and they go to
church on this day just as we do. In some provinces of
Canada they bake a special kind of bread at Easter time,
which probably stems from the old custom of always
baking a Good Friday loaf. This used to be called the Holy
Loaf, and it was kept throughout the year and used as a
remedy for all kinds of sickness and ailments. Pieces
would be crumbled from the loaf and used to make a
poultice for a wound that would not heal, or given as a
cure for any stomach upset. Many miraculous cures are
said to have been achieved with the use of the Holy Bread.

Easter Sunday

This day is better known as Easter Day, which commemorates the day that Christ rose from the dead. The churches are made very pretty at Easter time with lovely spring flowers, and there will often be new candles on the altar.

Another custom that is still observed by some people is the wearing of new clothes on Easter Day. It is not difficult to understand how this old custom first came about, because after the long fast during which devout Christians had often sprinkled their clothes with ashes to show repentance, they must surely have felt in need of clean new clothes.

This is also the day when children have chocolate Easter eggs, or sometimes Easter rabbits or hares. The shops are usually full of gaily wrapped chocolate eggs,

although many years ago it was the custom to have hard-boiled eggs with a colourful decorated shell. Sometimes the eggs would have tiny landscapes painted on them, or they might be boiled with the flowers of gorse and wild broom to dye them yellow or with a touch of cochineal which would turn the shells a deep shade of crimson. Another popular method of decorating eggs was to tie them in onion skins and then cover them with muslin while boiling them; this produced attractive patterns on the eggshells.

It is the custom to give eggs as presents at Easter because they are a symbol of new life – they are something out of which new life will come, in the shape of a bird. It is a pagan custom, and Easter itself takes its name from Eostre, the old Anglo-Saxon goddess of spring. The hare was sacred to Eostre, and ritual hare hunts took place at this time so that sacrifices might be made to the goddess. This is doubtless where the Easter bunny originated from. In Australia, children make Easter bunny nests in their gardens from twigs and moss, and then the parents put Easter eggs and chocolate bunnies into the nests for the children to have fun finding and collecting.

Pace-Egging
Pace-Egging is just one of the many different celebrations for Easter Monday, and still takes place in Preston in Lancashire. Children roll gaily coloured hard-boiled eggs down the slopes of Aveham Park on Easter Monday afternoon, and this is thought to be symbolic of the stone being rolled away from the tomb of Jesus.

Bottle Kicking and Hare Pie Scrambling

This is another Easter Monday activity that goes on in Hallaton in Leicestershire. It is a curious old custom but one that is always enjoyed by the local inhabitants. Many hundreds of years ago, an unknown person left a piece of land to the Rector of Hallaton with a rather strange request. Two large hare pies were to be provided, with two dozen loaves and a quantity of ale, and they were to be scrambled for.

What actually happens is that there is a church service in the parish church during the morning to bless the pies and the loaves. After this the Rector will cut up the pies and bread into small pieces, and put them into a sack. These are taken in the afternoon to a place known as Hare Pie Bank, with a procession leading the way, and then the pieces are scattered among the crowd and the people all scramble for them.

Preparations are then started for the Bottle Kicking session, although the bottles are in fact small wooden casks containing the ale. Two of them are filled with ale, while the third traditionally remains empty. (This probably adds to the fun of the game since it is no doubt difficult to know whether a cask is full or empty with such an uproarious game going on!)

Two teams of contestants take part, one team from Hallaton and the other from neighbouring Medbourne. There are no specified numbers for the teams, so each team may consist of any number of players. There are no set rules for the game, though it seems to be like a less complicated form of football. Each bottle is fought for in turn, and each team struggles to get the bottles or casks within its own boundary. The winners are the team that manages to get the two full bottles of ale, but usually after this hilarious contest is over the winners will share their bounty with the losers.

It was firmly believed by country people many centuries ago that the sun would actually dance with joy at the Resurrection on Easter morning. And it was traditional for country families to awaken each other very early on this day especially to see the sun 'dance'!

St George's Day

St George is the patron saint of England, and 23 April is celebrated as St George's Day. St George has been patron saint since the fourteenth century, and his special flag is a red cross on a white background.

Many churches are dedicated to St George, and one of the most famous is St George's Chapel at Windsor. There are many celebrations on this day to commemorate the saint, and one of them is a parade of the Queen's Scouts at Windsor Castle. They march through the streets of Windsor to St George's Chapel where a special service is held, and afterwards they march past the Queen who takes the salute.

There are many stories and legends about the bravery of St George and he is also the patron saint of soldiers. The most famous story of all concerning the saint is his adventure with a fierce dragon.

One day St George was travelling through a strange land, and he noticed that the people were all very sad and melancholy. He tried to find out why this was so and was told that a very formidable dragon lived just outside the walls of the city and terrorized all the people. Each day it demanded two sheep to eat, and now that there were no

more sheep or even cattle left in the city it had begun to eat the children and young people instead.

The people told St George that lots were being drawn each day to find out who should be the ones to go, and on this day the King's only daughter, who was very beautiful, had to be fed to the dragon. The king, beside himself with grief, had begged that his daughter be spared, but the people all agreed that it was only fair that she should go, for they had also lost their beloved sons and daughters. So the poor princess was sent outside the city walls to wait for the dragon to claim her.

When St George was passing that way he saw the beautiful girl standing there and was very distressed to think that she should have to die in this cruel way. He resolved to rescue her and waited with her until he heard the fearful snorting of the dragon. St George prayed to God for help and then rode bravely forward. As the dragon lunged towards him breathing out great clouds of fire and smoke, St George plunged his sword into the dragon and wounded it badly. Then he cried out to the princess, 'Hand me your sash, so that I may tie him up! Then you shall lead him into the city.'

But the people of the city were frightened and ran away in terror when they saw the dreaded dragon being led through the streets. St George had to put an end to their fears by killing the dragon then and there.

Before he left the city St George taught the people all about the Christian faith, and many were converted. The King was so grateful to St George that he wanted to give him a large fortune as a token of his gratitude, but St George would not hear of it. So the King built a church in the city and dedicated it to St George, saying that all the newly converted Christians could go there to worship God.

Shakespeare's Birthday

St George's Day is also William Shakespeare's birthdate, and he was born in 1564. (He is also thought to have died on 23 April, in 1616, but opinion differs about this.)

In Shakespeare's birthplace of Stratford-upon-Avon there are various celebrations on this day. Shakespeare was buried at Holy Trinity Church, and it is here that bells ring out in the early morning. Then there is a procession which starts at the famous Shakespeare Theatre and is led by a band and many prominent citizens, who all follow the route to the church. Here floral tributes are placed on the grave of this great British poet and playwright.

It is generally a festive day for Stratford, with the whole town looking gay with flags and decorations. Many of the streets are closed, and there is a special ceremony each year involving the unfurling of the flags of many nations. All this is done in honour of this famous man.

Anzac Day

New Zealanders and Australians celebrate Anzac Day on 25 April, and it is a public holiday in both countries. It is a day for remembrance of the landing by troops of the Australian and New Zealand armies on the Gallipoli Peninsula in Turkey, when an attempt was made to capture the peninsula during World War 1.

Gallipoli overlooks the Dardanelles, a strait which joins the Sea of Marmara to the Aegean Sea, thus separating Europe from Asia. The idea of the venture, which was carried out at dawn on 25 April 1915, was to open up the strait for the British navy and thus ensure the capture of Constantinople. The intention was to cause

Turkey to withdraw from the fighting, but this failed and many gallant Australians and New Zealanders were killed. So on 25 April the two nations remember and honour those who lost their lives in the battle, with services of remembrance held at cenotaphs and war memorials all over the two countries.

May

May is one of the most beautiful months of the year, and is named after Maia, the goddess of spring. The weather can often be very warm in May, and we think that summer has really come, but the winds can still be cold and in the past people were wary about changing from winter to summer clothing during this month. As the old saying tells us, 'Ne'er cast a winter clout till May is out'.

May Day
The first day of May has been an occasion for celebrating since very ancient times. We still have some May Day celebrations today, and in some country places there will still be a May Queen, and perhaps even a maypole.

Our ancestors treated May Day as a special day, with the young people getting up very early on this morning to go out into the woods and fields to gather the may-tree blossoms and greenery. It was lucky to bring home the first branches of may blossom to decorate the house, and a servant wishing to please her mistress would be sure not to forget this.

Fairs were held in many parts of the country, always starting on May Day but often continuing for a week or longer. There would be all kinds of things to eat – whole pigs and oxen roasted over huge fires in the streets – and pedlars and street criers would be there all selling their various wares. One of the best-known fairs and the biggest for miles around was held in a district of London that is still known to this day as Mayfair.

Maypoles used to be set up on every village green, and May Day was a holiday for everyone. The May Queen was always the prettiest girl in the village, and she was carried through the streets decked with garlands and attended by her maids of honour. If the village had no queen, a doll would be made and dressed like a queen and fastened to a long pole decorated with a garland and carried through the streets in the same way.

May Day at Padstow

At Padstow in Cornwall an old Celtic custom is revived each May Day using a hobby horse. This is a quaint creature made from a hoop covered with a black tarpaulin, which hides the legs of the wearer, and with a horse's head and a long straggling tail. It also has another head with a more carnival effect, being mainly a brightly coloured mask with staring eyes and a lolling tongue with sharp, snapping teeth. The 'horse' prances along the streets guided by a man known as the 'teaser' who carries a large club-shaped weapon which he waves backwards and forwards in front of the horse directing it on its rounds. Usually a small band will accompany the procession, and the horse is joined by other famous characters, such as Robin Hood and his men, and is also quite often joined by morris dancers.

The horse visits many houses on his merry round, and with the help of the band he will serenade the occupants with verses from a very old song called 'The Night Song'. Money is collected which in the past was used by the horse and his followers to buy beer from the inns they passed, but today is more likely to go to a local charity.

This merrymaking will go on for most of the day, with the hobby horse occasionally taking a young woman or girl out of the crowd and touching her lightly on the forehead with his hand. In years gone by, the hand used to be smeared with either soot or blacklead, and this action was thought to bring the person good luck.

One of the many old legends attached to this strange custom tells how around the year 1346 a French ship attempted to raid Padstow and sailed into the harbour. Unfortunately most of the local men were away fighting at the siege of Calais at this time, so there were mostly just women and children left. But they were resourceful, and as quickly as they could they made between them a huge and frightening-looking monster. They carried it to the harbour entrance, and the monster looked so evil and terrifying that the raiders quite thought it was the devil himself, and they fled leaving Padstow unharmed!

May Day in France

In France they have a very different sort of custom for May Day, in that lilies of the valley are always given to mothers and sweethearts. The flower shops will be full of these tiny flowers at this time of the year, and husbands and young men everywhere in France will buy them to take home to their dear ones. In country places these dainty flowers will often grow wild, so children are able to gather them for their mothers.

In other parts of the world May Day is celebrated in many different ways, and instead of May Queens and maypoles there are big impressive military parades. There will be labour meetings and political processions, and the old idea of rejoicing for the beginning of summer seems to be forgotten. But with 1 May now being a national holiday in Britain, maybe a few more old traditions will flourish again in this country.

Mother's Day

In Canada, Mother's Day is celebrated on the second Sunday in May, and Australians and New Zealanders celebrate Mother's Day around this time too. Children give their mothers chocolates, flowers or some other gift, and try to help in the home as much as they can to give their mothers a rest from the household chores.

In Australia the traditional Mother's Day flower is the white chrysanthemum, and the children give their mothers small sprays of the flower accompanied by a special card they have made at school. There are church services to celebrate Mother's Day in both Australia and

New Zealand, although in some parts of New Zealand the day is observed in March – around the time of our own Mothering Sunday.

Whitsuntide Festivals

Whitsun comes seven weeks after Easter, but the date varies as Easter is a 'movable feast' and so Whitsun must follow suit. If Easter has been late, Whitsun may fall in June.

Whitsun is one of the great festivals of the Church, and from Stuart times it was celebrated with much eating and drinking. A special kind of ale was brewed, which the Church wholeheartedly approved of as long as the congregation remembered to attend church. It was an old country tradition that the first gooseberries should be eaten at Whitsun, and that everyone should by then be able to enjoy the first digging of new potatoes. It was said that if you ate gooseberries on Whit Sunday you would be less likely to make a fool of yourself during the coming months than those who neglected to do so, who were bound to commit some sort of foolishness before the year was out!

There are several old Whitsuntide customs that are still kept up each year, some of them dating from pre-Christian days.

St Briavel's Cheese Ceremony

A curious little ceremony takes place at St Briavel's Church in Gloucestershire. After the church service on Whit Sunday, large baskets of bread and cheese are taken to a wall about three metres high adjoining the church, and a member of the clergy or a local forester will throw small pieces down to the congregation whilst they are leaving the church. There is a general scramble which ends when the baskets are held upside-down to show that they are empty.

This custom is said to date from the time of King John, and is connected with the rights granted by the king to the villagers, allowing them to graze their cattle and gather wood from an area of land known as the Hudnalls. This privilege was gained for them by the Countess of Hereford, who seems to have had to imitate Lady Godiva and ride unclothed through the village before this request would be granted. Ever since then the villagers have honoured their patroness by sacrificing some of their precious cheese, made from the milk of the cows on their new grazing land. At one time this was

given to the poor and aged, and even through the war years when cheese was rationed this custom was kept up. It is known as the Bread and Cheese Dole.

The Ram Fair

A Whit Monday festivity at Kingsteignton in Devon is the Ram Fair, which has a pre-Christian origin. Here the carcass of a young ram is paraded through the streets of the town, decorated with flowers and festive ribbons. As well as the parade there are sideshows and games and later in the evening there is dancing. The ram is then roasted and pieces are sold to the crowds.

The curious old legend attached to this ancient ceremony tells of a stream that supplied the village with its water centuries ago suddenly drying up for no apparent reason. Prayers were frantically offered to the gods, with every member of the village steadfastly praying, and their prayers were miraculously answered. A new spring was discovered one morning in the water meadows, and the villagers were so grateful that they at once offered up to the gods a tender young ram as a thanks offering. This custom has been observed ever since, and the new spring called Fair Water has apparently never run dry.

The Dunmow Flitch

This is another Whit Monday celebration that dates back at least to the thirteenth century. A high-ranking person in Dunmow, Essex, made a public offer that he would give a flitch (a whole side) of bacon to any happily married couple, provided that they could swear upon oath to having lived together peaceably for the space of a year and a day.

There is always a mock trial at which the couple must answer truthfully to all kinds of questions about their marriage. Today it is regarded as fun rather than as a serious business, but at one time the trial was conducted by the Prior of Little Dunmow himself, and woe betide anyone who tried to obtain the flitch under false pretences!

The donor of the flitch was said to have been 'heartily tired' of hearing his serfs and their wives nagging and bickering, constantly quarrelling and regretting their marriages. Whether this custom really did anything to solve marital problems is hard to say, but after a period when the custom lapsed it was revived and began to be regarded as a comic event, as indeed it still is today.

Dicing for Bibles

This unusual Whit Monday custom started around the year 1675 at St Ives, Huntingdonshire, when a certain Dr Robert Wilde left a sum of £50 in his will to ensure that some of the poor children of the parish should have a Bible. In accordance with the terms of the will the children had to throw dice for the Bibles, probably because there were so many poor children that there would not have been nearly enough Bibles to go round.

The will stated that the Bibles must be diced for in the church and that the dicing was to take place on the altar of the church . This was carried out until the year 1880 when a Bishop decided that it was not proper and moved the dicing to a table near the chancery steps. Today, however, the little ceremony takes place in the church school nearby. Six Bibles are diced for between twelve children, six belonging to the Church of England and the other six being non-conformists. Usually the Vicar is in charge of the proceedings, and quite a large crowd will gather to watch the dicing.

The Helston Furry Dance

The Furry Dance takes place in Helston, Cornwall, on 8 May, and the day is usually a holiday for most of the people in the little town. At one time anyone found working on this day was made to pay a fine or do a forfeit of some kind. A popular one was to make the victim leap the river at its widest part in one bound, which resulted in many duckings and caused lots of merriment.

The Furry Dance has a pagan origin, the word 'furry' thought by some to have come from the old Floralia Festival, and thought by others to be a relic of the Celtic Spring Festival. Its true meaning has never really been established.

Early in the morning both adults and children go out to gather wild flowers and branches of greenery, and this is called 'bringing the summer home'. The first dance begins as early as seven a.m., and used to be known as the servants' dance. The children's dance follows at ten o'clock, and then comes the important dance of the day, the noon dance. This is led by the mayor and other prominent citizens of the town, and the ladies are dressed in gay summer dresses, carrying flowers, whilst the men will perhaps wear morning suits with flowers in their buttonholes. The dancers pass in and out of the shops and houses, so the doors are left wide open, for this intrusion is firmly believed to bring very good luck to the occupants.

The dancing used to go on nearly all day and sometimes well into the night, but today the festivities will most often end with a dance for everyone in the evening. There has never been any known reason for the dances, but the people of Helston believe that it has something to do with St Michael, the patron saint of Cornwall.

It was said that on 8 May many years ago St Michael chanced to be out walking, when who should he meet but the Devil himself, who happened to be carrying a huge block of granite. Now the saint and the Devil were old enemies, and very soon they were disagreeing and fighting. The Devil, seeing that he was getting the worst of the conflict, dropped the huge block of granite and fled in a rage. Some say that he dropped the granite into the yard of a local inn called 'The Angel' at Helston, but others say that a small town grew up around the stone and as the stone had originally been brought by the Devil from the mouth of hell itself, the little town became known as Helstone. Either way it is believed that the Furry Dance was originally a celebration for those who managed to escape from the Devil's domain on the day that St Michael's action banished him.

Blessing the Sea
Also around this time in May, the old custom of blessing the sea takes place in Hastings, Sussex. This is an ancient rite going back to medieval days, and takes place in the evening around seven o'clock.

A procession of people, mostly fishermen and their families, leave All Saints' Church and the Church of St Clement and set off for the fish market. Here the Bishop of the diocese is waiting to give his blessing to the fishermen and their families, and to offer up prayers for a safe and successful season. All around the coast similar ceremonies are held at different times during May, and the boats and the nets are blessed too. In some places the clergy will even sail into the harbours to bless the water. Harvest of the Sea services are held each year in many churches near the coast, and the churches are often decorated with all manner of fishing tackle and nets. Fishermen have always been superstitious, and would never have dreamt of beginning the new season's fishing without the blessing of the priest, and without lighting a candle for their special saint, St Nicholas.

Oak Apple Day

There are various names for this day which takes place on 29 May, and in some country places it is known as Shig-Shag Day or Nettle Day, but it is most often known as Royal Oak Day or Oak Apple Day.

When Charles II claimed his throne in 1660 and made his triumphal entry into Whitehall on 29 May, it was exactly nine years after his lucky escape from Cromwell's men at the Battle of Worcester. The joyous people of England made this day a holiday, and there was much merrymaking and rejoicing. The oak leaf was generally adopted for the symbol of this happy day, because it was in an oak tree at Boscobel that Charles hid whilst Cromwell's troopers rode beneath the very tree.

Farm labourers would rise early to gather sprigs of oak to wear in their hats or buttonholes, and branches of oak leaves would adorn the door knockers of many cottages. They would then make a round of the richer houses in the country districts and bang on the door to demand beer or money to buy some. If they were refused and sent on their way they would shout out the words of this old rhyme as loudly as they could:

Shig-shag, penny a rag,
Bang his head in Cromwell's bag
All up in a bundle!

Founder's Day
Another ceremony that takes place on 29 May is known as Founder's Day. On this day the Chelsea Pensioners celebrate the birthday of Charles II, and there is a special parade of the Pensioners at the Royal Hospital, Chelsea. This is a reminder for everyone that Charles II was the founder of the hospital, and legend has it that he was urged to commission the building of this hospital by the famous Nell Gwyn.

The parade is usually inspected by a member of the Royal Family, and in the main court the statue of King Charles is decorated with oak leaves. All the Chelsea Pensioners wear sprigs of oak leaves on their scarlet jackets, and three rousing cheers are given for 'King Charles, our pious Founder'. Afterwards there is plum pudding and some extra beer for the old gentlemen.

June

In June summer has really come, and it can sometimes be very hot. The name June comes from the name of the Roman god Jupiter's wife, Juno, who was looked upon as the special benefactress of women.

There are not quite so many customs celebrated in June. This may be because people were far too busy with their crops and gardens at this time of the year to bother too much about feasting.

June is also the month of roses, and there are many other wild flowers in the woods and fields at this time. Poets are very fond of calling this time of year 'the leafy month of June'.

Father's Day

Some time around 20 June we celebrate Father's Day, which is not an old custom like Mother's Day but has only become popular in the last twenty years or so. Shop windows display special cards, and children will usually give their fathers small presents.

Father's Day is made more of in Canada, where there are quite often special family dinners cooked in honour of the day. Children often make their own cards at school, and everywhere the day is celebrated children try to take over one of the little jobs that father usually does around the house to give him a rest.

The Longest Day

The longest day is 21 June, and after this we begin to notice that the long light evenings will draw in just a little.

Midsummer Eve

Midsummer Eve comes next on 23 June, and it has in the past seen many strange old customs. (It was once called St John's Eve.) A pagan tradition was to light bonfires in many parts of the country, for people saw that the power of the sun noticeably decreased at this time of the year and they lit big fires in an attempt to help boost it a little.

This custom was strictly observed, especially in Cornwall, until the middle of the nineteenth century. Midsummer Eve was regarded as an enchanted time of

year, a time when witches and warlocks, fairies and evil spirits were at hand. Cornish people, who have always been very superstitious, would at this time light a chain of bonfires, placing them on all the headlands and furthermost points. The idea was to keep away all these evil influences and the fires would blaze all through the night, giving them protection. Young and old alike would join hands and dance around the fires, and when at last the fires grew low, newlyweds would often jump through the dying flames together. This was a good luck symbol for a new marriage.

Farmers drove their cattle through the dying embers of the fires to purify them, and to drive out any evil spirits. The ashes of these fires were always carefully collected, and when quite cold would be sprinkled on the fields to ensure that the crops would prosper. Or sometimes the ashes were kept to form the foundation for the next year's fires, and this was also considered to be a good luck charm.

At Stonehenge on Salisbury Plain another kind of ceremony is held on Midsummer Eve. It was originally a Druid ceremony to honour the Summer Solstice (which is 21 June, the longest day, as previously mentioned). A vigil would be kept up all night, and when the first rays of the rising sun shone on a stone known as the Altar Stone, the strange rituals would begin. Sometimes sacrifices were made to the sun god that they worshipped, and some of their practices were reported to be quite bloodthirsty. Today there is still a ceremony held at Stonehenge on Midsummer Eve. Many people of all ages gather there to watch the sun rise, but of course there is nothing frightening or gruesome about the ceremony now.

Here are a couple of old Midsummer superstitions.

Country people anxiously sought fernseed, which were thought to have magical properties, but were difficult to find. Fernseed are very tiny (they grow on the backs of the ferns, and are light brown in colour), and they could easily be lost on the way home. Anyone who found some and managed to keep them could, it was thought, become invisible, and this lucky person would then be able to watch unseen the revels and antics of the fairy folk, who were always very much in evidence on this enchanted evening.

Farmers hung sprigs of rowan tree over the stable and cowshed doors on Midsummer Eve, and anyone who had to travel by night tucked small sprigs of rowan into his horse's bridle. The rowan tree is feared by witches and all evil-doers, and is a charm against the evil eye.

Warrington Walking Day

On 28 June, a Walking Day is held at Warrington in Lancashire. This custom was started by a one-time Rector of Warrington in the year 1835, to draw attention to the Newtown and Latchford Heath Races that were held on this day each year. In his opinion these races caused much hardship and needless distress to the children whose foolhardy parents lost their money on the horses. The walks were an attempt to distract people from this expensive pastime.

Nowadays the races are long forgotten, but the annual walk still continues. The children of the town have a holiday from school so that they may take part if they wish. There is a procession through the streets led by a band, the children and supporters following carrying gay banners and flags. After the procession is over the churches have a short service, and the rest of the day will possibly be spent playing organized games, and treated like any other general holiday.

Walks seem to be more popular in the north of England than any other part of the country, and we hear of them in various towns. This may well be where the idea of sponsored walks first came from.

July

The month of July is named after the great Roman emperor, Julius Caesar. Our ancestors considered July to be the hottest time of the year, and it was often referred to as 'high summer'.

Dominion Day

In Canada 1 July is celebrated as Dominion, or Canada, Day, and is a national bank holiday when families set out to enjoy themselves. The day commemorates the founding of the country after the British North America Act of 1867 proclaimed a union of the provinces of Ontario, Quebec, New Brunswick and Nova Scotia. Other provinces gradually joined the union, and they became a dominion.

Some towns will have carnivals and parades with bands, and the children enjoy making their own fancy dress for these occasions at school with the help of their teachers and parents. In some cities the day is better known to the children as Firecracker Day, and there will be large displays in central parks or maybe on the beaches. These displays are strictly controlled, and children are never allowed to buy or set off fireworks without supervision. The reason for this is that at this time of year in Canada the temperature is often in the 80s or 90s and there is a great fire risk, especially in country areas. Forest fires are common, and authorities can expect to have at least a couple of dozen different fires burning in various parts of this vast country.

A great feature of many parades in Canada will be the Royal Canadian Mounted Police. They draw huge crowds in their colourful and spectacular uniform and are a magnificent sight.

Calgary Stampede

Between 3 and 12 July (or a period around that date) there is a big celebration held at Calgary in Alberta, Canada, known as the Calgary Stampede. This is a lively ten days of fun and entertainments of all kinds and is an exciting event that attracts huge crowds from many parts of Canada. There is plenty to see with noisy and colourful rodeos where cowboys battle with steers and bulls for large money prizes, and there are thrilling chuck-wagon races to watch.

The children have special days at this festival when they can take part in square dancing contests and get a free breakfast thrown in, or take a chance in the junior rodeos pitting their skills against the champions. There is always a big fair with many sideshows and stalls, lots of horse riding events to enter, and usually all the contestants enter into the spirit of the festival and wear true western costumes.

Indians play a big part in this great festival, and there is an authentic Indian village to wander through. Here many tribes combine to re-create their ancient folklore, and wear their traditional warpaint and costumes. Among the tall tepees and totem poles the original war dances are staged to a background of throbbing war drums and chants. It is a colourful and exciting spectacle.

Another big feature of the show are the cattle and livestock which the Canadian farmers and breeders bring

from all over the country to be either judged in competitions or sold.

The festival ends with a giant display of fireworks soaring high above the Stampede Park, which is a colourful ending to a great annual festival.

The Fourth of July

The American Declaration of Independence was drawn up on 4 July 1776, and it confirmed the colony's intention of breaking away from the British Empire altogether. This was during the six-year-long War of Independence, partly caused by disagreements over the right of Britain to tax her colonies and to interfere with their trading. The war and bloodshed and bitter feeling did not cease on 4 July, but the day has become a national Independence Day holiday in most of the United States.

There are many celebrations around the country, with some towns organizing big picnic parties and barbecues and others having colourful firework displays followed by dancing and parties. In many of the big cities there will be big parades with gaily decorated floats, and all the local organizations taking part.

St Swithun's Day

St Swithun's Day comes on 15 July, and, according to the old legend, if it rains on St Swithun's Day we shall have rain for forty days.

St Swithun's Day if it does rain,
For forty days it will remain,
St Swithun's Day if it be fair,
For forty days 'twill rain no more.

The legend of St Swithun is a very old one and was said to have taken place in the year 1100. (Sometimes you may see St Swithun's name written as Swithin – both are correct.) Bishop Swithun lived in the town of Winchester, and the people of the town all loved him very much because he was so good and kind to everyone. There are many stories of the wonderful things he did to help people in need, and here is just one of them.

One day an old lady was taking some fresh eggs in a basket to market to sell, and she had to cross a narrow bridge over the river to enter the town. The small bridge was crowded with jostling farmers and their men leading their cattle and livestock to market, and the poor old lady got rather roughly pushed about. The basket was knocked from her arm and the eggs spilled out and were broken. As she sadly bent to pick up the broken remains, Swithun, who was on his way to market and had seen what had happened, came to help her. He too bent to pick up the eggs, passing his hand over them as he did so. When he placed them back into the basket the old lady saw to her joy that they were all whole again. She was able to go to market after all and get a good price for her eggs.

Swithun was by nature a humble man and lived quite simply. He did not wish to have an elaborate funeral when he died so he left instructions about his burial. He wanted to be buried in a simple grave just the same as the ordinary people that he loved so well, and not in a costly tomb inside the cathedral like most bishops and important people. He wished his grave to be in the ground that lay outside the cathedral, so that he could have the open sky above him instead of the roof of a grand tomb.

So when he died the people of Winchester buried him as he had wished. They were pleased to do this because they felt that their beloved Bishop was still near to them, and they could visit his grave when they wanted to.

After several years had passed the Pope decided that Swithun should become a saint, and be known as St Swithun. The monks then living in Winchester became concerned about the saint's grave, for they felt that it was much too humble for a saint. They decided that the saint should be moved into the cathedral to a more fitting place, and the day of the removal was to be 15 July. A grand procession was planned, but unfortunately when the day dawned it was raining hard. By all accounts it rained so much that the procession was put off. Rain had never been seen like it before, and it became so very much worse that the monks were alarmed and uneasy.

The bad weather continued, and it rained for forty days without stopping. People began to say that God himself was not pleased with the monks' intention to move the saint from his chosen grave. It was rumoured that this rain was God's way of trying to prevent the removal, so the monks decided to leave the saint where he was.

Instead, they built a little chapel over his grave, making it into a small shrine for people to come and worship. Ever after this on 15 July people have remembered the legend of St Swithun and the rain. Some people say that if it does chance to rain just a little on this day it is God's way of christening the apples, and is counted as a blessing.

Klondike Days
Another big festival in Canada is celebrated around 20 July and takes place in Edmonton, the capital of Alberta. It is known as Klondike Days.

Edmonton, a beautiful city, owes its wealth and much

of its fame to the gold rush days of the late 1890s, and that is what Klondike Days remember. Before that time Edmonton was a quiet little town but it blossomed overnight with the sudden rush of thousands of families descending upon it, all heading north to the Yukon seeking their fortunes. Stores and shops of all kinds sprang up, industries grew and the town prospered.

Nowadays the people of Edmonton really enter into the spirit of the Klondike Days and dress in the manner of the 1890s. There are all kinds of events going on, such as carnivals with gaily decorated floats, bands and parades, horse racing and wrestling, and exciting stagecoach races. One special feature that everyone enjoys is the famous Great Tray Race where contestants all have trays loaded with foaming glasses of beer which must be balanced with one hand only.

It is also possible to try a hand at panning for gold, in true Klondike fashion, which is very popular with the children. There is also an exact replica of the Edmonton, Yukon and Pacific Railway for children to take rides on, and exhibitions of antique cars and model planes. It is possible to visit an old-time barbershop, an authentic gambling den, and a general store modelled on the goldrush days.

A highlight of the festival is the River Raft Race, which takes place on the fast-running Sourdough River, and hundreds and thousands of spectators line the banks to see some of the weirdest and wildest looking rafts imaginable. Every raft entered must be home-made and hand-decorated, and has to navigate ten miles of the river, which is no mean task. The two weeks are packed with fun and excitement, with lots of interest and lively entertainment for everyone.

Swan Upping

This very ancient custom takes place on the River Thames, on or about the last Monday in July every year. This custom was started during the reign of Elizabeth I, when it was necessary to obtain a royal licence to own a swan. The idea of the ceremony is to establish the ownership of the birds, and a convoy of gaily decorated small boats sets out from Southwark and sails up the river as far as Henley.

The little convoy is in the charge of the Queen's Swan Keeper, who wears scarlet livery. Two of the craft will be flying the Queen's Standard, and are followed by four craft that belong to the City Livery Companies. The Dyers' Company boasts a Swan Master, brilliant in blue livery, whilst the oarsmen wear gay striped white and blue sweaters with red woollen hats. The other Company, the Vintners', wears green livery and matching striped sweaters. These two companies alone have the right, which they share with the Queen, of being able to keep a 'game of swans' on the River Thames, between the waterways of London Bridge and Henley.

When the Swan Upping takes place, the cygnets are about two months old and each bird is caught and marked. The swans belonging to the Dyers are marked with a small nick on one side of the bill only, the Vintners' swans are nicked on both sides, and the unmarked swans belong to the Queen. It will take about a week to round up all the birds and mark them, because usually there are five to six hundred swans to be caught and examined.

Swans have always been regarded as 'royal birds', probably from the old supposition that Richard I brought the first swans to Britain when he returned from one of the Crusades. Since then, only those people obtaining a licence from the Royal Swineherd or having royal permission might keep them, and today they are still a protected bird belonging to the Queen.

August

August is the month of the harvest, and our Saxon ancestors called this month Arnmonat, *arn* being the Saxon word for harvest. It is usually a very hot month, and a favourite time for holidays in this country. In the old Roman calendar, August was the sixth month counting from March, and used to be called Sextilis (meaning sixth). But when the Emperor Augustus altered the calendar, he named this month after himself.

Lammas Day

The first day of August was known as Lammas Day, and in medieval times was an important day in rural areas because it marked the beginning of the harvesting.

The word Lammas comes from the old Saxon word *Hlafmasse*, meaning Loaf-Mass. At this time of the year it was a custom for housewives to bake loaves of bread from the freshly harvested wheat, and these loaves would be brought to the church to be blessed and to be used as a thanks offering for the good harvest at one of the many special services held during harvest time.

It was an old custom for farmers and employers to give their labourers and servants gloves at Lammas time, and many old records say that this had something to do with the rough work to be done at harvest time – cutting down the thistles and weeds that grew among the corn, for instance – where the gloves would provide useful protection.

So at the Lammas Day Festivals and Fairs gloves used to play a prominent part in the proceedings. At Exeter, for example, a huge glove was hoisted on a long pole and carried around the streets by the farm workers, finally coming to rest at the Guildhall where it would be fixed to the roof. This was a signal to everyone that the annual Lammas Day Fair with all its merrymaking had now begun.

Not many of the old Lammas Day celebrations still take place today, but one still in existence is the famous Doggett's Coat and Badge Race. This is often called the oldest rowing event in the world, and it takes place as near as possible to 1 August.

The race was started in the year 1715 by an Irish actor called Thomas Doggett, who was a Protestant and a dedicated supporter of the House of Hanover. To show his delight at the accession of George I he decided to give an annual prize to be rowed for each year by the London watermen. The prize was an orange coloured coat (today's coat is scarlet) and a silver badge, and when he died he left a sum of money to be invested so that the interest on it would pay for the annual prize each year, and the race might be continued for ever.

The race starts from the Old Swan Pier at London Bridge, and finishes at Cadogan Pier, Chelsea Bridge. It is a difficult race because the contestants have to go against the tide. A barge filled with supporters and past winners, all wearing their coats and badges, will follow the rowers.

(At this time in history the Protestants guarded the English throne jealously, fearing that the son of James II might succeed in gaining the throne of England and reinstate the Catholic faith, banning Protestantism forthwith.)

The Royal National Eisteddfod of Wales

The first week in August is an important week for the people of Wales, for it is the week of the National Eisteddfod. The Welsh have always been known for their traditional culture, and this is a great festival of the arts, poetry, music, singing, dancing, and other crafts; it is spoken or sung entirely in Welsh.

The Eisteddfod festival is very old, and it is recorded in Welsh history that Hywel the Good, a Welsh prince of the tenth century, had a special chair in his court reserved for the chief poet. The first Eisteddfod as we know it today was held in 1451, although there are references to the first Eisteddfod being presided over by King Cadwaladre in the seventh century.

The Eisteddfod is held in a different town each year, and on each day of the festival there will be some big event going on. There are choirs competing, soloist singers, all kinds of musical instrumentalists playing and the standard is very high with a great deal of work and effort going into each entry. The highlight of the great festival is the 'Crowning of the Bard', when the winning composer of the chosen poem receives the Bardic Crown. And then follows the ancient ceremony called 'Chairing the Bard'.

All the proceedings are watched over by a body of men and women known as the Gorsedd. They are all Bards, or musicians, or patrons of the arts, and they are appointed to see that the full ceremonials of the festival are properly carried out. There are three orders in the Gorsedd: the Ovates, who wear green robes, the Bards, who wear blue, and the Druids, who wear white. The Druids are the highest order, and are mostly men and women who have contributed outstanding work in connection with the fine arts in Wales.

On the Thursday afternoon the name of the winning Bard is announced, and the Archdruid will call upon some of the Bards to escort him to the platform, where he is chaired and then robed like the other Bards. The Archdruid then partially withdraws the grand sword from from its scabbard (the sword is a feature of Eisteddfod and has its own sword bearer) and cries out loudly, 'Is there peace?' and the huge crowd answer with one voice, 'Peace.'

On the Friday a very interesting ceremony is held when Welsh exiles from many parts of the world are welcomed officially to the festival. There are Canadians, Americans, Australians and many more, and for some it may be their first visit to Wales.

Schoolchildren perform traditional floral dances during this week, providing welcome interludes from the ceremonials. It is altogether a colourful and moving festival, and is attended by thousands of music lovers each year.

The Puck Fair
The Puck Fair is held in Ireland during the period 12–14 August, and it is an occasion for much fun and merrymaking. The fair dates back to long before the Middle Ages, and is surrounded by legends and stories that are still told to this day.

The fair used to be like a cattle market, with people bringing their cattle and livestock to Killorglin in County Kerry, either to sell or to exchange. Travelling tinkers and gipsies would be there all selling their wares, and there would be much drinking in all the inns. The fair today is different and on a much larger scale, with carnival sideshows, dancing, folk singing, and music of all kinds.

The curious name of the Puck Fair originates from the legend of the white billy goat known as King Puck. (He is now the toast of the fair, and is paraded through the streets on a float leading the carnival procession.) Many centuries ago certain high-ranking members of the Irish aristocracy decided to abolish this annual fair, complaining that the whole affair had got out of hand and that it had just become an excuse for drunkenness and wild behaviour. Troops were posted in and around the town of Killorglin at the time appointed for the annual fair, everyone was turned away, and the result was that there was much bitterness and tales of fighting and resistance. For three days and nights the troops kept guard, stemming the flow of people, most of whom had travelled many miles to be present at the fair.

On the eve of the third day when the troops were about to depart, secure in their minds that they had successfully broken the spirit of the fair, a remarkable discovery was made. There in the very centre of the market square, in spite of all their precautions, stood a lone man with a white billy goat. A notice hung round the goat's neck proclaiming, 'This goat for sale'.

Hoards of peasants, tinkers, and gipsies rushed in joyfully filling the square, shouting and declaring that the fair was open once more. The troops departed hastily for fear that the mood of the huge crowd should turn ugly, and this was how the Puck Fair survived.

There is another legend about the Puck Fair telling how

St Patrick himself had a hand in the origin of the white billy goat. If this story is true, then the fair is even older than we think. The saint and his followers are said to have been seeking new converts and they chanced to sail into a small creek near to Killorglin. The local inhabitants knew nothing about St Patrick and his teaching, so they rushed out wrathfully and drove the saint away as he tried to land. In vain did St Patrick try to explain, but no one would listen because they thought in their ignorance that he and his followers were invaders, bent on plundering and robbing.

At last the saint realized that his efforts were all wasted on these people, and he was heard to cry out in exasperation, 'Call yourselves Christians? Go and worship the goat, I can do no more!'

September

In the days of the early Romans September was the seventh month, and *septem* meant seven. The Emperor Augustus had a hand in changing the order of the months, but he did not alter the name accordingly.

The Harvest Home

Some time in September most country towns and villages will keep their Harvest Home festivals and celebrations. Today in churches all over the country such special services are held and the churches are made beautiful with flowers and sheaves of corn. Both the adults and the children of parishes will bring small gifts of fruit and vegetables to the Harvest Festival.

There is much legend and ancient tradition attached to the harvest, and some of the old rites and customs reach far back into pre-history. Country people believed that the 'Spirit of the Harvest' dwelt in the fields and she was thought of as the earth mother, Ceres or Demeter. And as the reapers cut the corn, so the earth mother was forced to retreat into the dwindling remaining corn. No one wished to be the one to cut the last row of corn, so they would take it in turns to throw their sickles and scythes at it until it was all down.

Then the women would enter the fields and gather up the remaining corn, taking it away to plait it into the shape of a female form, decorated with blue ribbons, to represent the earth mother. This would take the place of honour at the harvest supper table, and it may possibly have been the beginning of the corn dolly we know today. Many farmers would carefully preserve the straw image throughout the winter, and would plough it back into the earth in the following spring.

In some rural areas it is customary for farmers to leave a row of wheat standing in the fields at the end of the harvest, which you can sometimes see long after the rest has been cut. This is in accordance with the old belief that Ceres, the earth mother, lives in the fields, her spirit protecting the crops; by leaving a row of corn standing in each field the earth mother can make her home in it until the following spring.

Abbots Bromley Horn Dance

This very ancient dance is performed each year in Abbots Bromley, Staffordshire, by men wearing Tudor costume and carrying huge and very heavy reindeer antlers carved in wood and mounted on stout poles.

The dance takes place on the first Sunday after 4 September, and it lasts all day. There are six principal dancers known as the Hobby Horse, Robin Hood, Maid Marian, a Fool, the Man-Woman, and a Bowman.

The dance is thought to be of pagan origin, and one local explanation insists that the dance is a relic of an old hunting dance, and that this is why reindeer horns are used. Whatever its rightful origin, the Horn Dance has mainly survived because the Church made several alterations to the original dance, adapted it and gave it its blessing. In fact the horns are kept in the church where they hang on the aisle wall, and the costumes and other items used during the dance are kept in the vestry.

Maid Marian carries a curious collecting ladle, and the Fool has a collecting box. The proceeds of the day's dancing are always given towards the upkeep of the church. It is a processional dance led by the chief performers who make a tour of the district visiting various farms and houses on the way. The dancers are always made very welcome for they are thought of as luck-bringers.

There are no elaborate steps, most probably because the heads and antlers are so heavy to carry, but it is a very dignified dance. Every so often the dancers form a circle and perform a kind of set dance, dipping and retreating with the great antlers. Music is provided by an accordion player, and perhaps a boy with a triangle. The original music was always a pipe and tabor, and the old traditional tunes now seem to have given way to modern dance tunes.

It is interesting to note that although the carved heads of the animals are not thought to be more than sixteenth century, the horns themselves appear to be much older. The last reindeer in Scotland were well before the twelfth century, but like many of these very old dances and rites many theories are put forward, and all of them seem equally logical.

Clipping the Church

This very old ceremony takes place on the nearest Sunday to 19 September, and the church in question is at Painsworth in Gloucestershire.

Every year on this special Sunday a procession made up of the church choir, the children and people of the town, and the town band, make their way to the boundary of the churchyard. The children all form a circle around the church itself and dance round it. At intervals they go inwards towards the walls and then outwards again, which is called embracing the church and represents the love of the parish for its mother church.

Then a special Clipping sermon is preached from the stone steps at the foot of the church tower, and when this is over it means that the mother church has once again been 'clipped' (from the word *clypping*, meaning to clasp or embrace) for another year. This custom is a direct descendant from the pagan festival of Lupercalia, a tribute to Lupercus, the god of nature.

One of the old rites was a traditional dance around an altar, followed by the sacrificing of young goats and dogs. The eating of 'puppydog pie' is another relic of those days, but today a round cake is made with almond paste on top and a small china dog inside. It is a part of this ancient custom to remind us of the sacrificing, just as 'clipping' is a reminder of the age-old dance around the altar.

Viewing the Colours

Around 23 September the sun again crosses the Equator, and we have what is known as the Autumn Equinox, just as we have the Spring Equinox. Autumn begins now, and the nights get longer and the weather gets just a little cooler.

In Canada it is autumn too, but the Canadians call their autumn 'the fall'. It is traditional at this time of the year to go 'viewing the colours', for in the thickly wooded and forested areas the trees – especially the maple trees – turn beautiful shades of red and gold. Every 'fall'

hundreds of Canadian families will drive thousands of miles just to see these magnificent trees.

Michaelmas

Michaelmas Day is 29 September, and it is one of the four quarter days, the time when tenants and farmers usually pay their rents.

There is a wealth of old customs and traditions attached to this day, but not many of them still remain. The custom of eating Michaelmas goose on Michaelmas Day, however, is still carried on in many country villages and districts. This tradition derives from the quarter day itself, as an old rhyme tells us:

Whoso eats goose on Michaelmas Day,
Shall never lack money his debts to pay.

When the old farmers went to pay their rents at Michaelmas they often took with them a plump goose to soften the landlord's heart, especially if they were not able to pay their rents in full! Or perhaps it was just a crafty way of getting into the squire's good books because maybe a barn needed repairing, or their cottage had a leaky roof.

Another version of the Michaelmas goose tells how Queen Elizabeth I received the news of the defeat of the Armada on 29 September whilst she was sitting at dinner. She chanced to be eating roast goose at the time, so ever after on this memorable day it became the custom to serve roast goose.

The town of Kidderminster used to have a very curious way of celebrating Michaelmas Day until about 1845. It was the day when the town elected a new bailiff, and at a certain hour the town bell was rung – a signal that the Lawless Hour had begun. For the next sixty minutes the people of the town were allowed to throw debris at each other in the streets, such as apples and cabbage stalks or carrot tops. They really enjoyed this battle of rubbish throwing, and the fun was fast and furious.

At the end of the hour the bell rang again, and the throwing stopped. The new bailiff and his followers, members of the town council, came out of the town hall arrayed in their robes of office. They then walked in a procession to the house of the retiring bailiff to pay him their respects. But before they could enter his house a large crowd of people would be waiting for them at the entrance, ready to pelt them with more apples and cabbage stalks! There is no apparent reason for this strange old custom, unless it is a way of testing the new bailiff or just an excuse for the folks of the town to indulge in a little merrymaking at the town council's expense!

October

The Saxons used to call this month Wyn-monat, which means 'the month of the wine', because this was the time when everyone brewed their wines and malt liquors. It was also the time for fairs to begin, because the hard work of harvesting was over for another year and there were a few quiet weeks ahead before the long round of the farming year started again.

Mop Fairs

Until the First World War most towns and villages of any size had fairs at this time of the year and there were sheep fairs, horse fairs, the famous fig fair at Aylesbury, and, the most famous of all, the Hiring Fairs. Sometimes these fairs were known as Mop Fairs. This was because country people often changed their jobs at Michaelmas when some of the farms got new owners that the labourer perhaps did not like.

All the people seeking new employment would gather wearing or carrying the emblem of their trade. A milkmaid would carry her milking stool, the housemaid would carry a mop, the cowherd had a lock of cow-hair either in his hat or attached to his smock, and so on. As they stood in their groups waiting to be approached by the farmers and landowners, there was plenty to amuse them. All the street criers and pedlars would be there selling and crying their wares, and gingerbread men and gipsies selling gay ribbons and trinkets would be there too, jostling with travelling musicians who livened up the proceedings with gay tunes played on fiddles or flutes.

Horn Fairs

Horn fairs too were held in October. These were usually noisy and boisterous occasions, for this was the time that surplus cattle were killed off and sold by the local farmers to save them having to feed the cattle through the long winter months. People who bought the meat would salt it (which was the old way of preserving meat) and in consequence the horns became plentiful.

Roughly made horns were blown by the boys and young men of the fair, and stalls would be decorated with them. Farm workers all joined in the fearsome din of 'horn blowing'. Towards the end of the nineteenth century the old Horn Fairs died out, because modern methods of preserving meat and other foods were being devised and there was no longer the need for a sudden rush of slaughtered cattle.

Canadian Thanksgiving

Thanksgiving Day in Canada is on 11 October, and it is a national holiday for everyone. There are church services not unlike our own harvest festival services, with sheaves of wheat and lots of fruit and flowers decorating the altars. Children bring gifts to the church, and at home there are big family get-togethers.

It is traditional at this time to have roast turkey and cranberry sauce, followed by pumpkin pie. Families will travel hundreds of miles to be together for thanksgiving, and it is a great time for parties and for visiting friends and neighbours.

Old Michaelmas Day

On the same day, 11 October, it is Old Michaelmas Day, and this is worth a mention for the curious superstition that surrounds the blackberry. And surprisingly enough this old tale is well known all over the British Isles, even reaching as far as the Orkney Islands. It is supposed to be very unlucky to gather blackberries after this day, and this old belief arises from the medieval tradition that it was on this particular day that the Devil was banished from Heaven. He was thrown out with such force that he landed head first into a clump of blackberry bushes, and – as can be easily imagined – his temper was not improved. He trampled and spat on the offending bushes cursing them as he did so, and ever after this it is the belief that those who eat the fruit after this date will have sickness and perhaps even death in the family.

Trafalgar Day

Trafalgar Day is 21 October, and it commemorates the death of Horatio Nelson who died of his wounds on board the *Victory* at the Battle of Trafalgar in 1805. Nelson was a brilliant sea-lord, although his battle tactics were often completely unorthodox. He had a reputation for taking the enemy by surprise, with every move shrewd and well thought out.

Nelson was the son of a Norfolk clergyman, and he joined the navy as a midshipman when he was twelve. By the age of twenty he had become a commander. This great battle at Trafalgar, that cost Napoleon his fleet, proved to be Nelson's last. Just at the point of another brilliant victory, he was caught by the fire of a sharpshooter in the French ship *Redoutable* and musket ball penetrated his chest and remained lodged in his spine. He died about three hours later, at four-thirty in the afternoon.

So on Trafalgar Day each year in honour of this great sailor, his famous flag ship *Victory* (which is in dry dock at the Royal Portsmouth Dockyard) hoists the original signal. The signal Nelson ordered before the Battle of Trafalgar commenced was: 'England expects this day that every man will do his duty.'

Punkie Night

This is the last Thursday in October; it is a custom not often heard of nowadays, but Punkie Night still takes place in Hinton St George in Somerset. 'Punkie' is an old word for lantern, and these lanterns are made from hollowed-out mangelwurzels or swedes. They are

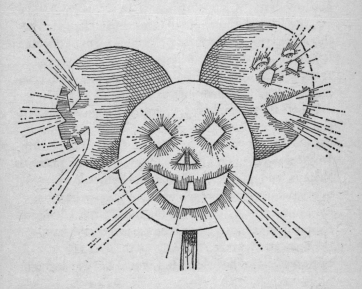

sometimes carved with patterns and weird designs, but they are most often cut to resemble ghoulish-looking faces with large grinning mouths, and they will have candles inside.

The children of this village go around together in groups walking through the streets. They sing a curious Punkie Song, and they knock on doors asking for money or for candles to put into their hollowed-out lanterns.

This is really an early part of the Hallowe'en celebrations. In medieval days these curious lanterns were always made at this time of the year, most especially in country districts where farmers would put a Punkie lantern on each of their gate posts. When it grew dark the small candle inside would be lit, to keep away witches and evil-doers.

Hallowe'en

Hallowe'en is the last night of October, and it used to be thought the most enchanted or haunted night of the year. It was the night when witches, hobgoblins, wizards and evil spirits came back to earth on purpose to weave their magic spells and enchantments.

Superstitious people kept up many strange old customs and rites in an effort to keep these evil influences away. Farmers would light big fires in their fields, and the farm workers and their families would parade around the fields chanting and singing old rhymes and hymns. At intervals the strange procession would stop to hear the local priest offer up prayers to the good spirits, asking for their help in the struggle to keep the evil ones at bay.

Great care was taken that none of the livestock or cattle was left in the fields. They would all be locked up securely in their stables and cow-sheds, and over each of the stable and barn doors a small bunch of rowan leaves would be hung. Witches and warlocks will not venture near the rowan tree, and with this in mind those who had to be out late on this enchanted eve made quite certain that they carried a small cross made from two twigs of rowan.

In more recent times Hallowe'en has become a time for parties, with children dressing up as witches and goblins and playing all kinds of special games such as ducking for the apple and apple bobbing. After the games there is often a big supper with plenty of pumpkin pie, gingerbread, spice cakes, and lots of other delicious things to eat.

Hallowe'en is kept up in many parts of Canada with many people giving parties. But for the most part the children will enjoy the fun of dressing up and playing the favourite game of 'Trick or Treat'. They run down each street knocking on the doors crying loudly, 'Trick or Treat', and most people will have a treat of candy or sweets ready to give them. Those that do not can expect maybe to have a trick played upon them, such as a tyre being flattened, or windows being soaped, or just knocking on the door and running away.

Most of the children carry plastic shopping bags with them to store their 'treats' in, and organized groups from schools will usually carry collecting boxes for Oxfam or some other deserving charity. The children are dressed as ghosts, goblins, witches, or anything ghoulish and suitable for Hallowe'en. Many of the houses will have a jack-o'-lantern in their windows, which are hollowed-out pumpkins with candles burning inside them. But in this modern age many of the pumpkins are being replaced with plastic electric ones that can be brought out each year. This is an American idea.

One old superstition is often practised at Hallowe'en by young girls anxious to know the name of their future husband. An apple has to be peeled carefully without breaking the peel, and then the peel must be thrown over the left shoulder where it should land in the shape of the initial letter of the name of the girl's sweetheart.

Another similar superstition but more especially for older spinsters is that at midnight on All-Hallows Eve the spinster must stand before her mirror, and by the time the clock has finished striking twelve a vision should appear beside her own face in the mirror. It will be the face of her future husband.

Nowadays these old superstitions are paid very little heed, and the old idea of ghosts and witches and evil spirits being abroad on this night has long since gone. But they make a very interesting part of our ancient folklore.

November

November was the ninth month in the old Roman calendar, and it took its name from *novem*, meaning ninth. This is often a very damp and misty month, and we sometimes get frosts. If the frosts were very hard farmers used to believe that this foretold a wet dreary winter.

Frost in November
Enough to hold a duck,
All the rest of the winter
Will be nought but slush and muck.

All Saints' Day

The first day of November is All Saints' Day, when the Church commemorates all the martyrs and saints who died for the Christian faith. This festival began in the seventh century to commemorate a great religious event, the conversion of the Pantheon – the Roman temple dedicated to all the pagan gods and goddesses. The early pagan temple built some years before the birth of Christ was destroyed in a terrible storm. But the Emperor Hadrian replaced it, and for several hundred years it was devoted to the worship of numerous pagan gods and goddesses. When at last Rome became converted to the Christian faith, the temple was used for Christian worship. It was dedicated to Mary, the Mother of Jesus, and at a later date dedicated to all the other martyrs and saints.

All Souls' Day

This day follows All Saints' Day, and is the day that the Church sets aside for remembering ordinary people. The commemoration of All Souls' Day used to begin on the night of All Saints' Day, and a strange custom was enacted. The poor people of the towns and villages would go begging from door to door for 'soul cakes', which were a kind of flat, spiced bun. Church bells would ring out on this evening telling everyone when 'souling' had begun. A curious old song known as the 'souling song' was sung as the soulers went begging from door to door:

Soul, soul, for a soul cake,
I pray thee good mistress a soul cake.
One for Peter, two for Paul,
Three for the One who made us all.

There were several more such verses to this song, and quite often the wealthier people would invite the soulers into their homes to give a full rendering of it.

The custom of souling seems to have originated from an older tradition when the poor people of the towns and villages went round to their richer neighbours begging for food, and was carried on until the beginning of this century. Because of their superstitious beliefs in spirits and the evil eye, they thought it only right and proper that a feast for the dead and buried must be held on the night of All Saints' Day. So on this night it was the custom in many homes to set the table with food and to leave the door of the house wide open so that the spirits of the dead might enter. No one wished to be present when the spirits came, so the feast was always set late at night, for the dead to feast to their hearts' content while the occupants of the house slept peacefully.

In Ireland this old custom was also kept up and it was usual for a candle to be put in at least one window of each house. This was done in order to guide lost and earthbound souls, and it was thought that the light would help and cheer them as well as guide them to the feast with all the other spirits of the dead.

No doubt the flat spiced soul cakes were given in place of other foods in later years because souling must have proved quite expensive even for the rich.

Guy Fawkes' Night

Guy Fawkes' night on 5 November is still a very popular custom in this country. Some families still have bonfires in their gardens, but on the whole there is a tendency to have bigger displays of fireworks in a central place such as a park, so that everyone can enjoy the fireworks but they are kept under supervision.

The man who started all the celebrations was Guy Fawkes who, in 1605, with other Catholic conspirators, plotted to rid themselves and the country of the then King, James I, and his Parliament. They planned to do this by exploding thirty-six barrels of gunpowder under the Palace of Westminster, which is now known as the Houses of Parliament. They chose 5 November because this was the day that the King proposed to open Parliament, and it was a time when they could be sure that all the members of Parliament would be there too.

The conspirators rented the house which adjoined the House of Lords and made a tunnel from the cellar of the house to enable them to gain an entry into the vault of the House of Lords. This took nearly a year, but finally thirty-six barrels of gunpowder were secreted there and

covered with a pile of firewood. On 4 November Guy Fawkes (who had been chosen because of his experience with explosives while a soldier, and because he was unknown in London) went down into the vault to begin his lonely vigil.

But the plan was destined never to take place; the conspirators were betrayed when a Catholic peer received an anonymous letter telling of the plan. Immediately a search was made of the cellars and vault, and Guy Fawkes was discovered hidden away with the barrels of gunpowder, with his tinder box and matches at the ready. He was arrested and thrown into prison, and with his collaborators was executed in January 1606.

Ever since this unfortunate happening, Parliament has always been thoroughly searched before each annual opening.

After the event the Church ordered prayers of thanksgiving on every following 5 November, and gradually as the years went by it became part of the celebration to have bonfires. The custom of having a 'guy' on top of the bonfire became popular, and Guy Fawkes became immortal.

In the seventeenth century bonfire night was the scene of great revelry and wild practices. Huge fires would be lit in the streets, started from blazing tar barrels that were rolled up and down the streets. It became very dangerous indeed to be out in the streets on this night, and many houses were burned in consequence.

Fortunately regulations came into force forbidding the burning of tar barrels in the streets, and people began to have much smaller bonfires in their own gardens. Bonfire night became a more festive occasion, and when the fires burned low potatoes were cooked in the red-hot embers, and sausages were toasted on sticks. An old Norfolk custom was to roast chestnuts in the ashes at the end of the evening and serve them piping hot with glasses of delicious raspberry vinegar or ginger ale.

There is a Guy Fawkes rhyme that used to be chanted by children pushing their home made guys around the streets on old prams or carts, as they begged a few coppers to buy fireworks from passers-by:

Please to remember,
The fifth of November,
With gunpowder, treason and plot.
I see no reason,
Why gunpowder treason,
Ever should be forgot!

In Australia children are told the old story of Guy Fawkes on 5 November, but fireworks are banned because of the bush-fire danger. It is the beginning of summer in Australia at this time.

The Lord Mayor's Show

The Lord Mayor of London's Show is always held on the second Saturday in November, and it is a very colourful sight as the new Lord Mayor drives in splendour through the streets of London in an elaborate gilded coach. There are coachmen and attendants in livery, and the fairytale-like coach itself, with its painted panels and shining gilt decorations, looks magnificent as it is drawn by six horses. This state coach was built around 1757; it weighs nearly four tons, and it is not considered to be very comfortable to sit in as it was built long before the use of springs became widespread!

The Lord Mayor's Show is one of the best-loved London customs, and it dates from the year 1215. This was when King John decided that each Lord Mayor must be approved by the reigning monarch himself, and if the king could not be present then he must be presented to the Royal Justices. In the very early days the Lord Mayor rode on horseback attended by his men. Sometimes the custom was varied and he travelled up the Thames in a state barge. Since 1712, however, he has ridden in a coach and the pomp and splendour of the procession and the ceremony has never altered.

The Lord Mayor proceeds to the Law Courts to take his oath of office before the Lord Chief Justice, and when this ceremony is over the procession will return along the Embankment to the Mansion House. Thousands of people line the route each year to watch this colourful spectacle, and to speed the new Lord Mayor on his way.

Remembrance Sunday

On the nearest Sunday to 11 November there will be Remembrance Services held in churches throughout Britain in villages and towns alike. It is the day when everyone pauses to remember those who lost their lives in the two World Wars of this century.

In almost every town and village there are war memorials, erected in memory of all the local men who died fighting for their country. In London there is a large memorial called the Cenotaph in Whitehall, and each Remembrance Sunday a big ceremony is held there. Many wreaths are laid at the foot of the Cenotaph, with the Queen placing the first wreath of poppies followed by many more from various statesmen and members of the forces.

At eleven o'clock in the morning, while this ceremony is taking place, there is a two-minute period of silence, a short pause whilst everyone stops to honour the dead of the two World Wars. This hour was decided upon because it was at eleven o'clock in the morning on 11 November 1918 that the First World War ended.

The poppy is the symbol of this day, and millions of poppies are made and sold in the week before Remembrance Sunday. They are made by disabled ex-servicemen of the British Legion. The idea of making artificial poppies was first thought of by a French woman, Madame Guerin, who noticed how tragically but inevitably the blood-red poppies bloomed on those battle-stained fields in northern France. Her idea caught on, and in 1922 the British Legion's first poppy factory was opened. It provided work for many disabled ex-servicemen, and this was of course every bit as vital as the money that the sales of the poppies realized.

In Canada, Australia and New Zealand the people there treat Remembrance Day in the same way, with memorials and ceremonies the same as ours, for many thousands of their men also died in the two wars. In Canada it is the custom for everyone to put their poppy in a remembrance garden near to the memorial or perhaps on a tomb commemorating nameless thousands who died for their country.

Thanksgiving Day
Thanksgiving Day is celebrated throughout the United States of America on the last Thursday in November. For the American people this is a special day, for it commemorates the first harvest festival held by the Pilgrim Fathers at New Plymouth in the year 1621.

The voyage of the Pilgrim Fathers on their ship the *Mayflower* was hazardous, but they overcame their difficulties and reached the American coast of New England (although they had been aiming for Virginia, which was further south). They settled where they landed, and when they had survived through a terrible year they celebrated with a feast of the food which was plentiful.

At this first harvest festival roast turkeys were eaten, because turkeys were so plentiful in that particular part of New England. And so today American families will still have roast turkey, usually served with cranberry sauce, and have pumpkin pie to follow. This is a time for most families to get together and celebrate with parties, and there are special thanksgiving services in the churches of some states.

St Andrew's Day

St Andrew is the patron saint of Scotland, and we celebrate St Andrew's Day on 30 November. This saint is rather special because he lived in Galilee at the same time as Jesus. He and his brother Simon Peter were fishermen, and they were two of the first men that Jesus chose to work with him.

It was Andrew who discovered the small boy with the five barley loaves and two small fishes, when Jesus fed the five thousand who had gathered to hear him preach. Andrew was a great preacher himself, and he converted many people to the Christian faith and founded many churches.

St Andrew was not a native of Scotland even though he is Scotland's patron saint. He became the patron saint around the middle of the eighth century, after his relics had been brought to Scotland. There is an old story that shows how Andrew became Scotland's patron saint, telling how the saint had angered a Roman senator whilst he was preaching in Rome. He had managed to convert the Senator's wife to the Christian faith, and once she was converted she wanted her husband and family to follow the new faith as well. Andrew was arrested, and the Senator ordered him to be put to death in the most agonizing way he could think of. And so, like many of the saints and martyrs, St Andrew was crucified, but not in the usual way nailed upright to a cross. He was bound to a cross made in the shape of the letter X, and this form of crucifixion was a much slower and more lingering death.

Many years later his remains were taken to Constantinople to be buried there, once Christianity was the recognized religion of the great Roman Empire. And then a man called Regulus, who was the keeper of the graves, had a very strange dream. He dreamed that an angel brought him a message, telling him to take the remains of the saint and to journey with them until he found a safe resting place for them. He did the angel's bidding, and after several years of wandering about he came to Scotland. Another dream told him that it was here that he must bury the saint's remains.

The place where he buried the saint later became known as St Andrews.

St Andrew's Day is a very festive time for Scottish people, and they have big reunions and celebrations wherever they are in the world. The dinner and celebrations on this day usually start with the old Scottish tradition of piping in the haggis. This is followed by many highland dances and Scottish reels, and it is a merry occasion that often keeps going for most of the night.

December

This month is most probably the best-loved month of the year, especially with children, for it has Christmas Day as its outstanding celebration.

But before Christmas Day itself there are one or two interesting old legends and celebrations that lead up to Christmas as we now know it.

St Nicholas's Day

The feast day of St Nicholas is 6 December, and it is a European festival for children. St Nicholas was a bishop of Myra in Asia Minor, but he is better known to everyone as the patron saint of children. (Although St Nicholas actually lived in the fourth century, many of the customs associated with him started much later.) In many parts of the world children hang up a stocking on Christmas Eve for St Nicholas to fill with sweets and toys. (In some parts of Europe children hang their stockings on St Nicholas's Day.) St Nicholas is often called Santa Claus, Father Christmas, or even St Nick – but no matter which name is used, he is one and the same person.

St Nicholas was very fond of children and young people, and he was especially patient with them, taking time and trouble to teach them Christian beliefs and to help them in every way. But like most of the saints he was persecuted for his good deeds and for the teaching of the Christian faith, although he is remembered for his generosity and kindness.

There is an old legend about St Nicholas which may well show the beginnings of the tradition of hanging up a stocking on Christmas Eve. In the town where St Nicholas lived, there were many poor people. Some of them were so poor that parents even sold their children as slaves. One family in particular known to the saint became so destitute that in desperation the father made arrangements to sell three of his daughters, because that way he could manage to provide for the rest of his family.

When St Nicholas heard about this he went at night to their home, and threw a bag of gold coins through an open window. The gold was intended to save the eldest daughter from slavery, and the next night he repeated his visit and so saved the second daughter from the same fate. A third visit secured the safety of the last of the fated daughters, but by now the saint's generosity had become known. This was thought to have started the giving of gifts to children on the eve of St Nicholas's Day, but in much later years this custom was transferred to Christmas Eve.

It is also a custom on St Nicholas's Day to elect a Boy Bishop, and this is still done in some parts of England such as Edwinstowe in Nottinghamshire, Par in Cornwall, and at Pokesdown in Hampshire. This old ceremony goes back to the ninth century, having started originally after the murder of three young boys.

A wealthy nobleman sent his three young sons to Athens to receive education, and on their way he had instructed them to call upon the Bishop of Myra (St Nicholas) whose good deeds and fame had spread far afield by then. The three boys reached Myra very late one evening and decided to put up at an inn for the night. The inn-keeper was a greedy man and saw the rich garments that the boys wore and noticed that they were carrying bags of gold coins. So whilst they slept he murdered them, and cut up their bodies into pieces and hid them in a large barrel of brine.

But he had reckoned without St Nicholas, for the saint had a vision that night in which he saw the whole wicked deed. He arose at once and went to the inn demanding to see the inn-keeper. He confronted the frightened man and accused him of the three murders, and the inn-keeper was so terrified that he begged for mercy and confessed his guilt. St Nicholas prayed to God for a miracle, and prayed that the three murdered boys might be restored. His prayers were answered, and the boys – so the old legend goes – rose up from the barrel, their severed limbs whole and sound again. The saint then blessed them and sent them on their way to Athens.

To commemorate this deed and the subsequent miracle, the custom of electing a Boy Bishop to rule over the churches from St Nicholas's Day until 28 December (the Day of Holy Innocents) came into being. The Boy Bishop used to wear episcopal vestments and took part in all the services which did not require an ordained priest. He would lead processions through the streets collecting alms for the poor, and on his last day of office he would preach a short sermon. If he should die whilst holding this special office, he would be buried with full honours, and with as much pomp and ceremony as befitted a real bishop.

Today's Boy Bishops are usually choir boys, and although they wear all the attire and robes of a bishop, they do not take part in the actual services.

St Thomas's Day

St Thomas's Day is 21 December, and on this day at a place called Old Bolingbroke in Lincolnshire, a curious old custom is observed – they hold a candle auction. This event used to take place every five years, but now it is an annual event.

It concerns a piece of land known as Poor Folks' Close, and it belongs to the Church. But it is auctioned annually, no doubt as part of the deeds or will of whoever bequeathed the land. It is an interesting ceremony usually carried out by the vicar or a member of the Parish Council. The auctioneer sticks a pin into a tall tallow candle about an inch or so from the top, then the candle is lit and the bidding begins. The idea is to be the last bidder so the bidding is fast and furious until the flame reaches the pin and it drops out, and then no more bids are accepted. So the last one to bid before the pin falls becomes the new tenant of the land for a whole year. All the money collected is given to the poor and needy of the parish.

Another old St Thomas's Day tradition called Going a Gooding used to be carried out by the women and girls of each town and village. They went from house to house, begging from their richer, wealthier neighbours either food or money to help provide for the Christmas feast. In return for the provisions or money a large bunch of holly and mistletoe would be left on the doorsteps of those who had given generously.

This old custom has long since gone, and the Christmas bunches are seldom seen now, although they were probably the forerunners of the gay holly wreaths that many of us hang on our doors at Christmas time.

St Thomas's Day is also the shortest day of the year, and after this day the days will gradually begin to lengthen. Old country people would often begin to plant various crops on St Thomas's Day, thinking that seeds so planted would be bound to prosper under such a saintly influence, and would similarly increase in size with the lengthening hours of daylight. Ale brewed on this day was thought to be extra good, and likewise the meat from pigs or cattle killed on this day. Even the day's baking was thought to come under this same saintly benevolence.

Christmas Day
Christmas really means the mass, or the festival, of Christ, and although it cannot be certain that Jesus was actually born on 25 December, this was the date agreed upon as the celebration of his birthdate.

Christmas Day is celebrated in many parts of the world, and most of the celebrations have a similarity. Nearly everywhere children believe in Father Christmas, and they hang up a stocking to receive gifts on Christmas morning. One of the loveliest of Christmas customs is the Christmas tree, and we bring it into the house and decorate it with tinsel, baubles and coloured lights. The origin of the Christmas tree is believed to be German, brought to this country in 1841 by Prince Albert, the husband of Queen Victoria. He set the tree up in Windsor Castle, and decorated it with sweets and tiny gifts for the royal children. Ever after this it became the custom to have Christmas trees in the house at Christmas time, and by the middle of the last century there were hundreds of trees for sale at Covent Garden. A very large one was erected at the Crystal Palace, not unlike the

enormous tree we have each year in Trafalgar Square which is a gift from the people of Norway.

There is an old German legend which tells how the spruce tree became the first Christmas tree. One very cold December night, a holy man called St Boniface, who lived in the eighth century, was walking through some woods. He came upon a group of people worshipping a pagan god, and they were about to sacrifice a small boy to the god when the saint managed to convince them that their beliefs were wrong. He took an axe and felled a mighty oak – a tree that was sacred to the pagans. When they saw that it fell to the ground with no ill effect, they took heart and listened to the saint. He told them the story of the Christ child, and led them to where a small fir tree was growing, saying, 'From this night, the little fir tree shall be your holy tree. It is a sacred tree because the wood of the humble stable that sheltered the Christ child was also from the fir tree.'

Carol singing plays a big part in the Christmas celebrations, both in churches and around the streets, as well as on the radio and television. And in many schools a nativity play will be acted by the children, reliving the story of the Christ child. The schools are often gaily decorated with evergreens and paper chains, and also with the cards that people have sent to each other. Christmas is a family time when people get together to have one big celebration. People send cards and presents to their families and friends, and the cards make good decorations around the house.

In many large department stores throughout the world there is a Father Christmas, and at most children's parties around this time the highlight of the evening is the appearance of that same merry old gentleman.

Different parts of the world celebrate in different ways, although the spirit of Christmas is the same everywhere.

In Canada many families will have a Christmas tree on their front porch, twinkling with gay coloured lights as a welcome for guests. Often the lights extend to the gardens to decorate the smaller trees and shrubs. At their big family parties they eat the traditional Christmas fare of roast turkey, cranberry sauce, and rich plum pudding. Because the Canadian climate is so different from ours, they can almost be certain that there will be quite deep snow at Christmas time. The children make snowmen, and they also make snow angels by finding a stretch of untrodden snow to lie on and then moving their outstretched arms up and down and their legs together and apart. In this way they form the imprint of an angel.

In America only Christmas Day is celebrated, and the children think of Father Christmas as St Nick. They hang up stockings or pillowcases in the same way as English children do, and there are all the usual festive trimmings about the houses. Christmas dinner will more likely be roast beef or Virginia ham instead of roast turkey, because it must be remembered that they have just recently celebrated Thanksgiving with turkey and cranberry sauce.

But in Australia Christmas is quite different because the temperature there is somewhere in the 90s. Many families look forward to Christmas as the start of their annual holiday period, and many people spend Christmas Day on the beach, with a picnic Christmas lunch.

It is hot in Mexico, too, so the children are able to make small cribs of moss and stone in their gardens, with stone figures of the Nativity. And the children in Mexico band together to go from house to house asking for sweets or some small Christmas token. Most families have something ready for this regular Christmas custom.

In France the children will often leave their shoes in the fireplace for Père Noël to fill with small toys and sweetmeats. Most French families will have a model of the crib and small presents will be left beside it for the children of the family.

Candles play a very prominent part in Norway and Sweden at Christmas time. Norwegian families light candles on Christmas Eve, and it is the custom to let them burn through the night to guide the Christ child. The candles are blown out in the morning, but they are re-lit every evening until New Year's Day.

Swedish festivities hail from the old festival of Saint Lucia. Each village used to select a Saint Lucia for the year, and the chosen girl would wear a white dress and a scarlet sash. Upon her head she would wear a crown of lighted candles, and it was the custom for her to ride out of the village and visit all the outlying farms and houses. She was said to bring them the promise of good fortune and prosperity. The modern modified custom from this is for most families to light a candle in the window, to show that they have remembered the Christ child's birthday and to hope that the house will be blessed.

Many Christmas customs have disappeared from Russia nowadays, but one particular legend is still told to children at Christmas. It concerns Baboushka, who was one day visited by the Wise Men, who were journeying from the East to Bethlehem, guided by the light of the wonderful star. They sought food and refreshment from Baboushka, and she made them very welcome. She asked them why they travelled by night, and they told her that they were going to see the Holy Babe at Bethlehem and must travel

by night because the bright star was their only guide. Baboushka asked if she too might go along, and the Wise Men agreed, saying that she must leave with them that night, because they feared the bright star might disappear.

Baboushka was very houseproud, and she stayed behind after the departure of the Wise Men to tidy up her home, saying that she would catch up with them. But by the time she was ready the star had gone, and all trace of the Wise Men with it. Baboushka eventually reached Bethlehem, only to find that Mary, Joseph and the Holy Babe had fled to escape from Herod, and the old legend goes on to say that to this very day Baboushka still searches for them at Christmas time.

Boxing Day
Boxing Day on 26 December is really St Stephen's Day. St Stephen was the first saint to die for preaching the Christian faith, and he has the honour of having his day next to Christ's birthday. St Stephen's Day became known as Boxing Day back in the Middle Ages, because it was the day when the priests of each parish opened the poor boxes which were always kept in the churches.

Today we still have boxes in our churches, and we put money in to help with the upkeep of the church. In the past there were many very poor and needy families who were in need of food and clothing, and so at this time of year the boxes were opened for them.

Christmas boxes originated from this custom, too, for in later years it became the custom for wealthier people to give their servants a gift of money on this day. The money was given in small boxes, but nowadays we just give the money to tradesmen and the people who have served us well through the year just past.

Boxing Day in Ireland has a very different meaning, and is still called Wren Day in many parts. On this day up until the middle of the last century groups of boys and girls dressed in fancy dress parade around the streets of the towns. They would chant verses of the old Wren Rhyme, accompanied by musical instruments of one kind and another.

The wran, the wran, the king of all birds,
St Stephen's Day he was caught in the furze,
Although he is little, his honour is great,
So rise up kind sir and give us a 'trat'.
We have followed this wran ten miles or so,
Through hedges and ditches and heaps of snow,
We up with our wattles and gave him a fall,
And so brought him here to show you all.

One of the boys would be carrying a Wren Bush – a few branches of evergreen tied to a long pole, and a small box dangling from the pole. In the box there would be a small effigy of a wren. This is all part of the custom, but the wren these days is most likely a toy one, or even just a small bunch of feathers. These little birds are no longer hunted, but in the past whole villages would turn out to hunt the wrens.

And why was the wren so hated and persecuted? There are various reasons, but a popular story put forward tells that when St Stephen was being sought by his enemies he hid himself away. But his whereabouts was soon discovered because a small wren flew about chattering and calling out his secret to his enemies.

Another old tale tells of some Viking raiders who were

bedded down for the night in a camp when a party of Irish warriors crept up on them thinking to surprise them in the early hours before dawn. But the raiders were alerted by a small wren who tweaked and pecked at them to awaken them, and thus they escaped with their lives. Ever since that day, the old legend tells us, the Irish have always hated the wren.

Boxing Day in England will often bring a visit to the pantomime or perhaps the circus, or maybe there'll be a trip to an ice show – just something good to round off the Christmas celebrations. Cinderella, Peter Pan and Dick Whittington are familiar figures at these kinds of shows, and all are a part of the traditional Christmas festivities.